Rescuing Sadie

Also from Susan Stoker

Badge of Honor: Texas Heroes Series

Justice for Mackenzie
Justice for Mickie
Justice for Corrie
Justice for Laine
Shelter for Elizabeth
Justice for Boone
Shelter for Adeline
Shelter for Sophie
Justice for Erin
Justice for Milena
Shelter for Blythe (June 2018)
Justice for Hope (Sept 2018)
Shelter for Quinn (TBA)
Shelter for Koren (TBA)
Shelter for Penelope (TBA)

Delta Force Heroes Series:

Rescuing Rayne
Assisting Aimee (loosely related to this series)
Rescuing Emily
Rescuing Harley
Marrying Emily
Rescuing Kassie
Rescuing Bryn
Rescuing Casey
Rescuing Sadie
Rescuing Wendy (May 2018)
Rescuing Mary (Oct 2018)

Ace Security Series:

Claiming Grace
Claiming Alexis
Claiming Bailey
Claiming Felicity

Rescuing Sadie

By Susan Stoker

A Delta Force Heroes/Masters and Mercenaries Novella

Introduction by Lexi Blake

EVIL EYE
CONCEPTS

Rescuing Sadie
A Delta Force Heroes/Masters and Mercenaries Novella
Copyright 2018 Susan Stoker
ISBN: 978-1-945920-82-0

Published by Evil Eye Concepts, Incorporated

Sign up for the 1001 Dark Nights Newsletter
and be entered to win a Tiffany Lock necklace.

There's a contest every quarter!

Go to www.1001DarkNights.com for more information.

As a bonus, all subscribers will receive a free copy of
Discovery Bundle Three
Featuring stories by
Sidney Bristol, Darcy Burke, T. Gephart
Stacey Kennedy, Adriana Locke
JB Salsbury, and Erika Wilde

An Introduction to the Lexi Blake Crossover Collection

Who doesn't love a crossover? I know that for me there's always been something magical about two fictional words blending and meeting in a totally unexpected way. For years the only medium that has truly done it well and often is comic books. Superman vs. Batman in a fight to the finish. Marvel's Infinite Universe. There's something about two crazy worlds coming together that almost makes them feel more real. Like there's this brilliant universe filled with fictional characters and they can meet and talk, and sometimes they can fall in love.

I'm a geek. I go a little crazy when Thor meets up with Iron Man or The Flash and Arrow team up.

So why wouldn't we do it in Romanceland?

There are ways out there. A writer can write in another author's world, giving you her take on it. There's some brilliant fanfiction out there, but I wanted something different. I wanted to take my time and gradually introduce these characters from other worlds, bring you in slowly so you don't even realize what I'm doing. So you think this is McKay-Taggart, nothing odd here. Except there is…

Over the course of my last three books—Love Another Day, At Your Service, and Nobody Does It Better—I introduced you to five new characters and five new and brilliant worlds. If I've done my job, you'll know and love these characters—sisters from another mister, brothers from another mother.

So grab a glass of wine and welcome to the Lexi Blake Crossover Collection.

Love,

Lexi

Available now!

Close Cover by Lexi Blake
Her Guardian Angel by Larissa Ione
Justify Me by J. Kenner
Say You Won't Let Go by Corinne Michaels
His to Protect by Carly Phillips
Rescuing Sadie by Susan Stoker

Acknowledgments from the Author

When I got the call last year asking if I wanted to "play" in Lexi Blake's sandbox, I immediately said, "Yes!" But then reality set in...I knew how popular Lexi's Masters and Mercenaries series was—in part because I was reading it before I started writing my own stories. I asked Lexi if she had a female character I could "have" and of course she said yes. And thus Sadie's story was born.

I've loved everything about the process of writing this novella and the following story is typical of what I write...strong heroines who seem to get into the worst situations...but luckily they have attracted the attention, and love, of an amazing, Alpha, possessive Hero who will do whatever it takes to make sure she's safe.

I hope you enjoy Sadie's story...and getting to know (or see again) some of the characters from my Delta Force Heroes series. Read on!

Chapter One

Sadie faced the man in front of her without trepidation.

Sean Taggart might know twenty ways to kill without making a sound thanks to his time as a Green Beret, but to her, he was just Uncle Sean. She'd only known him for six years, ever since Aunt Grace got married, but he'd always supported her no matter what she wanted to do and treated her and her aunt Grace like princesses.

Not this time.

"Uncle Sean, this is ridiculous."

Sean crossed his arms, giving her what she knew was his "displeased" face. Brows drawn, lips pressed together, eyes narrowed. "It's not and you know it."

"Why can't I just go back up to Dallas with you?"

Her uncle sighed. They'd been over this before, but Sadie couldn't let it go.

"Because Jonathan is still missing. Captain Jackson said he'd continue to look after you until he's caught."

Sadie shook her head. "But if I came home, *you* could keep me safe."

Sean looked down at her with love in his eyes. His voice gentled. "I could, you're right. But I think we both know that you wouldn't like my kind of protection. Or Ian's. Or anyone else we could find."

She knew what he meant without him coming right out and saying it. Sean was overprotective. As was Ian, and probably most of the other men who worked for McKay-Taggart. She could handle their overprotectiveness and bossiness…but only to a point. If she had to endure it twenty-four seven, it could damage their relationship. And that was the last thing she wanted.

"I can go stay with Milena's parents again," Sadie volunteered almost desperately. Maybe she'd even make it in time for Milena's surprise engagement party. She might not want to become one of McKay-Taggart's overprotected clients, but she wasn't sure she wanted to be in close quarters with Chase Jackson anymore either.

From the second she'd laid eyes on the man, she'd wanted him. It was as if her body had said, *This is it. This is the man I want.*

Unfortunately, he'd been in the middle of rescuing her from a crazed, perverted pedophile at the time, and now she was afraid he felt responsible for her, rather than wanting her back.

She'd been staying with him, sleeping in the extra bedroom in his apartment, but things were extremely awkward between them, mostly because of their crazy sexual chemistry. Then their friend TJ, a San Antonio highway patrolman, had called and said the FBI had gotten word of a sighting of Jonathan Jones recently. Now Chase thought that moving her to an apartment over a friend's garage would be safer. Sadie felt as if she were a foster kid being pawned from one home to another, not actually belonging anywhere.

"Milena's man can't take care of both you and her," Sean said bluntly, responding to her earlier thought about staying with her friend's parents. "TJ's got his hands full making sure Milena and his son are safe. Not only that, but if you went back to San Antonio and stayed with Milena's parents, you'd put them in danger. Look, I know you and Chase don't get along all that well, but you just need to continue to put up with him until we can find that asshole Jones and make sure he's no longer a threat."

Sadie swallowed. It wasn't that she and Chase didn't get along; she simply didn't know what to say to the man. She liked him. A lot. And every time she opened her mouth, she said stuff she didn't mean. But if she kept protesting, Uncle Sean would get suspicious and ask questions. The last thing she wanted was her uncle, and Chase, to know how much she really *did* like the gorgeous Army captain.

Some of her trepidation must have shown on her face anyway, because Sean said, "You'll be safe with Jackson, Sadie. If he didn't already belong to Uncle Sam, I'd be recruiting him to come work for Ian in a heartbeat. Besides, thanks to the media, Jonathan knows who I am. Who *you* are. The first place he's gonna look for you is in Dallas."

"So you're continuing to pawn off the babysitting job to Chase,"

Sadie said bitterly.

The look in his eyes wasn't one she'd had directed at her often, if ever. Disappointment. And it hurt. Especially coming from Uncle Sean. "You are not a babysitting job," he said. "And the fact that you even said that tells me you really don't understand the seriousness of this situation."

"I'm sorry," Sadie said immediately. "I do understand. I just… I don't think Chase likes me very much and I hate being a burden."

Sean looked at her for a long moment with an expression on his face Sadie couldn't interpret. Finally, he said, "Sometimes I forget how young you are. The fact of the matter is, right after you were rescued, Jackson came to *me* with the request to keep you safe. I didn't ask him."

Sadie stared at her uncle in disbelief. "He did?"

"Yeah, he did."

"But…he was so mad at the school after he helped me. I didn't think he wanted to be anywhere near me."

"Can you blame him? He was worried about you. We all were," was her uncle's simple response.

"It's already been a month. How long am I gonna need to be down here?" she asked, referring to Fort Hood, where Chase lived and worked.

"As long as it takes. Please do this. For me and Grace. We need to know you're safe while we track this asshole down. It shouldn't be for very much longer."

When he asked nicely like that, how could she keep protesting? "Fine."

"Thank you."

"But don't blame me if Chase calls you up, begging you to take me off his hands."

Sean smirked at her, as if he knew something she didn't, but didn't respond. Instead he enveloped her in his arms and held her tightly for a long moment.

Sadie closed her eyes. Sean was a big man, and Sadie had always loved his hugs. Being in her uncle's arms made her feel as if nothing could hurt her. He and the others at McKay-Taggart had been worried when she'd up and left for San Antonio without really telling anyone where she was going and for how long. But when she'd called and told them she was going to stay with her friend, Milena, and help her with her toddler, Sean hadn't read her the riot act, which she appreciated. Sadie hadn't planned on being involved in a bust at Milena's workplace, the Bexar County School and Orphanage for Girls, and afterward, she couldn't leave, not when it was clear Milena might be in danger because of Sadie's involvement.

Of course, she hadn't known she was also in danger until it was too late.

The only other time she'd felt this safe was at the school…after Chase had hauled her into *his* arms.

Sean pulled back and held her at arm's length. "You know I'm always a phone call away. You need me, you call." It wasn't a question, more of a command.

Sadie nodded.

"And if you want a job at the restaurant when you come home, it's yours."

"Thanks, Sean," Sadie said. Her uncle's restaurant, Top, was one of the most popular restaurants in Dallas. Working there wouldn't be a pity job either; it would be hectic and busy. If she couldn't get her job back at McKay-Taggart, it would be a good option for her.

As if Sean could read her mind, he said, "Ian told me that things haven't been the same since you left. He's actually gotten his phone messages and can see the top of your desk."

Sadie chuckled and playfully smacked his arm. "Shut up. I wasn't that bad."

Sean simply looked at her with his eyebrows raised.

"Okay, fine. I was. But I got the job done and was damn good at it. Besides…they got the important messages, didn't they?"

"That they did," Sean agreed. The grin left his face and he said somberly, "Be safe. You have a lot of people who love you."

"I will," Sadie told her uncle.

"I'm prouder of you than I can say. Not many people would stay to try to help a friend they hadn't seen for a couple of years. Not only that, you were instrumental in getting that child-abuse ring stopped and taking down a lot of sick men who were involved."

Sadie's eyes filled with tears. She didn't realize until right that moment how much she needed her uncle's praise. She hadn't thought she'd be in danger when she'd gone down to San Antonio. All she'd wanted to do was visit Milena and her little boy for a while. She'd gotten in over her head, but luckily TJ, Milena's new fiancé, was not only a badass cop, he was also a former Delta Force sniper who'd been able do what needed to be done when the shit hit the fan.

Hearing her uncle, who was a badass in his own right, tell her he was proud of her, went a long way toward helping Sadie forgive herself for the worry she'd put her family through, and was *still* putting them through.

"Thanks," she murmured.

"But if you do anything like that again, I'll have Ian find a safe house to stash you in or put guards on your ass twenty-four/seven. And I'm not kidding."

Sadie's eyes widened and she looked at her uncle in shock. Would he really sic bodyguards on her? Yeah, he totally would.

Before she could respond, even though she had no idea what she might say, Chase Jackson stuck his head into the small room at the police department, where Sean had met them. They had discussed Jonathan and had been updated on the search for him.

Other than the reported sighting of him down in San Antonio, which had prompted Chase's decision to move her to his friend's garage apartment, there hadn't been any other updates. With every meeting, Sadie got more and more frustrated. The man was a master of disappearing into thin air. But she'd thought that before, and it had turned out Jonathan and his now-deceased, equally perverted father, Jeremiah, had been lurking in San Antonio the entire time, waiting for the perfect moment to make their move against Milena and her son, as well as Sadie.

"Everything okay?" Chase asked, obviously having seen her surprise at her uncle's last words.

Sadie looked over at him.

He was really good-looking. Dark hair and brown eyes that always stared at her with an intensity that made her want to squirm. He filled out his clothes in a way that hinted he was one big muscle underneath them. She wanted to run her hands up and down his body to feel his muscles for herself, but so far had refrained.

Chase was also a couple inches taller than she was. She hadn't always been attracted to tall men, but spending time around her uncle and his friends had changed that. She always felt protected when they were near. Part of it was because of what they did, but it was also watching them with their wives. They'd tuck their women under their arms, or pull them against their sides, or push them behind their own bodies if they thought there was a threat.

Sadie hadn't ever had a boy, or man, protect her like that. Then again, she'd never really *wanted* to be protected. But watching Sean, Alex, Ian, Liam, Jake, and Adam with their wives gradually made her realize she might be missing something. Having someone constantly be looking out for her well-being wouldn't exactly be a hardship.

And Chase had certainly made her feel protected. The second she'd run into him in the school after escaping Jonathan, she'd gone from being scared out of her mind to being surrounded by Chase's manly scent, and it had calmed her.

But Chase could also be super confusing. Running hot and cold. One minute she was sure he wanted her, and the next he was treating her as an annoying little sister. The last month had been torture, being around him and not knowing what he really thought about her.

The old Sadie would've called him on it. But ever since being held captive by Jonathan Jones at that school, she'd felt unsure about nearly everything. She hated not being the kick-ass Sadie she used to be and was working her way back to being that person, but it was slow going.

"I was just saying goodbye to Sadie," Sean said, turning away and bending over to pick up Sadie's bag. "Grace packed some stuff for you," he told his niece, handing her the bag. "Thought you'd appreciate having more of your own things."

Sadie nodded. She wasn't surprised Aunt Grace had the presence of mind to make sure she had more of her favorite clothes. Every time her uncle had come to check on her, he'd brought more and more of her wardrobe. Before long, Grace would have sent her entire apartment. As it was, it already looked like she'd completely moved in with Chase.

"Take care of my niece," Sean ordered Chase.

"She'll continue to be safe with me," Chase replied.

The two men stared at each other for a long moment. Finally, Sean nodded. "I'll be in touch."

Then he leaned over, kissed Sadie on the head, and was gone.

She turned to Chase and held her bag in front of her like a shield.

He held out his hand. "Ready to go?"

Sadie swallowed hard and nodded. She put her hand in his and let him lead her out of the small room.

Chapter Two

Chase Jackson tried to keep his eyes off of Sadie's ass as she climbed the stairs to the apartment over Cormac Fletcher's garage, but failed. He was only human, after all.

The first moment he'd seen Sadie Jennings, he'd wanted her. Wanted her with an intensity that seemed to come out of nowhere. He hadn't ever felt like this about a woman before. As if he needed her in order to breathe.

"Are you sure it's okay for me to stay here?" Sadie asked as she put the key in the lock.

"Us."

"What?" she asked, a confused look on her face.

"Us," Chase repeated calmly. "And yes. Fletch has no problem with *us* staying here while your uncle and the Feds continue to try to track down Jonathan."

Sadie froze—one hand on the doorknob and the other holding her bag as if her life depended on it. "I thought you'd just be with me during the day."

Chase gently edged Sadie to the side and pushed open the door. He put his hand on the small of her back and guided her into the apartment. He pried the bag out of her hand and let it drop to the floor before leading her into the living area, which contained a couch, a small coffee table, and a television.

"Chase?"

"I can't make sure you're safe if I'm not here, Sadie."

"But...your Delta Force friend lives next door. I thought that's why I would be staying here," Sadie protested.

"That's part of why you'll be safer staying here. Not to mention the cameras he's got covering every inch of the property. But if you think I'm going to rely solely on him or the cameras to keep you safe, you're crazy." Chase turned to look at the woman who'd had his feelings turned upside down since the day he'd met her.

She was looking at him in confusion, chewing on her lower lip, her brows furrowed. She was also wringing her hands in front of her and she wouldn't *quite* meet his eyes. He wanted to shake her at the same time he wanted to haul her into his arms and tell her she never had to worry about anything ever again.

Her auburn hair hung in curls around her pale, freckled face. He loved how her small upturned nose wrinkled when she was confused and how her face glowed pink when she was embarrassed or excited. Her eyes were a hazel green that sparkled when she spoke of anything she was passionate about...which was almost everything. She was tall, around five-nine, and curvy. Her hips were wide and she had a small pooch of a belly, which was cute rather than a turnoff. Her arms and legs were muscular; he knew from talking with Sean Taggart that when she lived up in Dallas, she worked out at least twice a week with the men and women in the McKay-Taggart group and held her own.

But it was more than her looks that drew him. It was her personality. She was loyal, both to her friends and her family. She was determined and compassionate. She was tough, fearless, and most of the time not afraid to speak her mind.

Sadie looked around the small apartment. "There's only one bedroom."

Chase wanted to tell her that they'd share it, but didn't want to make her uncomfortable. "I'll sleep on the couch."

Sadie looked at it dubiously, then looked him in the eye. "I'm not a baby, Chase. I'll be perfectly fine here by myself. You can go back to your place to sleep, then come here in the mornings if you feel the need to babysit me."

"Let me make something perfectly clear, Sparky, the last thing I think about when I'm around you is babysitting. You're what, twenty-five? Only two years younger than me?"

"Yeah," she answered reluctantly, hating that she'd thrown the same words at Chase that she had her uncle. "But you act a lot older," she told him defensively when he didn't say anything.

Chase grinned at her. Fuck, she was cute.

"And don't stand there smirking at me," she huffed, crossing her arms over her chest.

The smile left Chase's face. "I've seen a lot," he told her quietly. "Too much. So much that there's no way I'm going to leave you here to fend for yourself when that asshole is out there, dying to get his hands on you. That is in no way baby-fucking-sitting. I can protect you, Sparky. Make no mistake."

"Why are you calling me that?" she asked, instead of commenting on his over-the-top statement.

"What...Sparky?"

"Yeah."

Chase grinned. "Red Hair. Explosive personality. Fire. It fits you. I like it."

Sadie stared at him for a long moment before rolling her eyes. "You think I've never heard that one before? Newsflash, I've been called every name under the sun related to red hair. Chucky, Copper Top, Red, Carrot Top, Rusty, Fire Crotch—that one by an asshole at college, who thought he was God's gift to women and was pissed I wouldn't give him the time of day—Red Riding Hood, Pippi, Annie, and even Garfield. Sparky isn't even that creative, all things considered."

Chase took a step closer to her, and she took a step backward before squaring her shoulders and glaring at him. He reached out a hand and tugged on one of her curls. He let the piece of hair wrap around his finger before slowly palming the side of her head with his large hand. He smiled at her. "I'd never disrespect you by calling you something derogatory. Sparky is an endearment, and a compliment. You don't take crap from people, and the passion I see burning inside matches the color of your hair. Both are beautiful, and I respect the hell out of you."

"Oh."

Not taking his hand from the side of her head, Chase leaned into Sadie, close enough he could smell the jasmine lotion she'd used that morning. "Anything else you need me to clarify?"

Her eyes were huge in her face as she stared up at him. She stood stock-still, as if afraid to move. "Why are you doing this?" she whispered. "You don't even like me."

"Not like you?" he asked incredulously. "Is that what you think?"

She nodded. "I heard you telling my uncle on the phone that I was impulsive, and not in a good way. You also said it was stupid of me to keep going to that school to assist Milena after I had my suspicions about what was happening there. You told him that he sure hadn't taught me anything in the time I'd worked for McKay-Taggart, even if I was only the receptionist."

"Yeah?" Chase asked, sounding unconcerned.

"Yeah. And you even told him that you thought I needed a 'keeper.'"

When she didn't continue, Chase asked, "You overhear anything else?"

Sadie shook her head slightly, her hair still caught in his fingers. "No. I left after that. I decided I'd heard plenty."

"You didn't eavesdrop long enough, Sadie. You didn't hear me tell your uncle that, for someone who hadn't been trained, you had a remarkable innate ability to know what to do in an emergency situation, and I was fucking impressed."

Her mouth dropped open and she stared at him in shock.

"Or that, while you might have been irresponsible by continuing to go to work with Milena, I thought you were incredibly brave to have blown the whistle on the operation in the first place, and then continue to go there to protect her, even when you had a pretty good idea what was happening to the girls behind the walls of that hellhole."

Sadie's mouth closed with a snap.

"I like you, Sadie Jennings. I might not always like the things you do, but I do understand why you're doing them. That it's just who you are."

"You like me?"

Chase wanted to grin, she was so fucking adorable, but he didn't. "Yeah, Sparky. I like you. I like you enough that the thought of Jonathan getting his hands on you makes me physically ill. I've spent the last month getting the approval of my commanding officer to make you my official job. To make sure you're safe. The weapons stockpile the Feds found in the secret tunnels of the school was enough to get that approval. RPGs aren't the kind of weapon the average citizen should have at their disposal. So, while your uncle, his friends and brothers, and the FBI track down Jonathan and eliminate the threat hanging over you, I'm going to keep you safe. With help from Fletch, Ghost, and the others."

"This is ridiculous, Chase. I'll be fine up in Dallas. Uncle Sean will make sure I'm safe," Sadie told him. "Watching over me twenty-four seven has to have gotten old."

Chase tightened his hand in her hair. "It hasn't."

Sadie sighed in frustration. "I'm putting you out. I'm in the way. Let me go home, Chase."

His countenance gentled, but he still shook his head. "Jonathan was going to rape you, Sparky. You said so yourself. You told the Feds that he was obsessed with getting you pregnant and taking your babies for himself. Do you honestly think he's going to just give up and run away with his tail between his legs?"

She bit her lip and looked away from him.

Chase could see that she knew Jonathan wasn't ever going to stop looking for her. The man was obsessed. Chase also knew that Sadie had tolerated staying at his apartment with him only because she thought Jonathan would be found right away, and because it would keep Milena and her son safe at the same time.

"I can take care of myself," she protested.

"Let me do this," Chase said in a low tone.

"Why?"

"I don't think you're ready to know why," Chase told her.

That obviously got her hackles up. "I might be younger than you, and not an officer in the Army, but I'm not a baby. I have my concealed handgun license and have learned a lot from working at McKay-Taggart. I'm not a victim either. I'm not going to cower and cry and wait for that asshole to find me. What aren't you telling me?"

"You want to know why I don't want you to go back up to your badass uncles? Back up to Dallas, where they have an entire team of men who could keep you safe? Because yeah, I know they could."

Chase waited for her to nod before continuing. He leaned closer and his hand moved to the side of her neck, holding her still. His lips brushed against her right ear as he proceeded to rock her world.

"You may not have thought I liked you before today, but mark my words, Sparky—you're *mine*. And I'm personally going to make sure that asshole is wiped off the face of this earth so he can't look at what's mine anymore. So he can't touch what's mine. So he can't even *think* about what's mine. Then, when he's dead, I'm going to marry you—and spend the rest of my life making sure no other asshole thinks he can do the same thing."

Sadie gulped and shifted in his grasp. She didn't say anything, just stared at him in shock as he pulled back from her. His hand still rested on her neck and he could feel her pulse hammering in her throat. His eyes roamed over her, taking in her peaked nipples and the lust in her eyes.

"Now, are you going to let me keep you safe, or do you want to run away and hide behind your uncles?"

"I'll stay." Her words were more of a croak than actual syllables.

He smiled...and couldn't help the relief that coursed through his veins. "Good."

"I don't do well cooped up," Sadie warned him, stepping back from his hold.

"I'm not your jailer," he responded immediately, letting her retreat. "I didn't say we would have to stay in the house every minute of the day. As long as there's no obvious threat, we can hang out with my sister and her friends, go to the grocery store, things like that, as long as it's within reason."

"As long as I don't have to just sit around," Sadie grumbled.

"We don't have to just sit around...unless you want to."

Chase barely kept himself from leaning forward and taking her lips with his when her cheeks pinked. He didn't know exactly what she was thinking, but he could guess—because it was exactly what *he* was thinking he wanted to do. Their chemistry was off the charts. His gaze dropped to her mouth, imagining how her lips would feel against his for what seemed like the thousandth time.

"I...I should probably unpack," she mumbled. "See what my aunt put in the suitcase this time for me."

"You do that," Chase said, not taking his eyes off her lips.

She licked them, and every muscle in his body clenched, a split second away from pulling her into him and not letting her go until they were both gasping for air. But now wasn't really the time. He needed to keep his wits about him. Keep her safe. He took an additional step back, putting a foot of space between them.

She glanced up at him, as if trying to read his mind, then scooted off to the side and toward the front door, where he'd dropped her bag when they'd entered the small apartment. Chase watched as she hurried to the door of the bedroom and disappeared inside.

He ran his hand through his dark brown hair and tried to ignore his rock-hard cock. Living in close quarters with Sadie was hell. He would've liked to have kept her in his apartment. In his space. In his bed. But he knew she'd be safer here, where Fletch could help him keep an eye on her. He tried to tell himself that eventually, she'd be moving back to his apartment with him…by choice.

He hadn't lied. He wanted Sadie Jennings. Wanted to marry her. Wanted to tie her to him so tightly she not only wouldn't *want* to let him go, she wouldn't be able to either. He wanted her more than he'd wanted almost anything before in his life.

He just hoped Sean Taggart didn't feel the need to castrate him when he found out how closely he was guarding his niece's body.

Chapter Three

Sadie was in the kitchen of the small apartment making lunch, trying to avoid Chase and figure out exactly what was going on between them, when he came in to help her. The kitchen wasn't big enough for the two of them, but he didn't seem to notice...or care.

When she turned to open the fridge, she bumped into his chest. He put his hands on her hips and smiled at her as he said, "Excuse me."

Three minutes later, when she reached for the handle of one of the cabinets to grab a plate, Chase was there, his hand covering hers as he gently pushed her out of the way and got it down for her.

Minutes after that, when he put his hands on her hips and moved her aside so he could get to the sink, Sadie'd had enough.

"Chase, this kitchen isn't big enough for the both of us. I got this. Go...sit or something."

He tightened his fingers, and Sadie swore she could feel his thighs against hers. "I wanna help, Sparky."

"It's only sandwiches," she said, clenching her eyes tightly closed and praying he'd step away before she did something stupid, like turn around and throw herself at him. "Maybe you can check with TJ and see how Milena is doing?" she asked, trying to think of something he could do *outside* the kitchen.

"I can do that," Chase said quietly. Then he leaned close and whispered in her ear, his warm breath against her neck sending goose bumps racing down her arms. "I like mayonnaise on my sandwich."

Shit, she was so screwed. Her body reacted as if he'd said he wanted to rip her clothes off and take her right there in the kitchen, instead of telling her how he wanted her to make his lunch.

She couldn't get his earlier words out of her mind.

You're mine. And I'm personally going to make sure that asshole is wiped off the face of this earth so he can't look at what's mine anymore. So he can't touch what's mine. So he can't even think about what's mine. Then, when he's dead, I'm going to marry you—and spend the rest of my life making sure no other asshole thinks he can do the same thing.

The words were just as shocking now as they'd been before. He hadn't done anything inappropriate since, and hadn't brought it up again. But the space he'd been keeping between them when she'd been at his apartment was gone. He been touching her constantly since he'd declared she was *his*. Brushing his shoulder against hers. Touching her hand with his when they walked next to each other. If she was honest with herself, she had to admit she loved his touches, although she wasn't sure how she should respond, and that left her confused.

Sadie nodded stiffly to his comment about mayonnaise and held her breath until he backed away and his hands dropped from her hips.

It wasn't until he'd left the kitchen that she let out the air she'd been holding. She finished the sandwiches before heading out of the kitchen. She put the plate with Chase's sandwich on it next to his right elbow and went to sit on the other side of the small table.

"Sit here," Chase ordered, not harshly. "I want to show you what TJ sent." He gestured to the open laptop in front of him.

Reluctantly, knowing she hadn't had enough time to shore up her defenses against him, Sadie put her plate down and pulled a chair closer. The delicious smell that emanated from Chase filled her nostrils, and she tried to tamp down her body's reaction. Leather and peppermint.

The leather was easy to understand, because of the jacket he'd taken off when they'd arrived at the apartment. But the peppermint was harder to explain. She hadn't seen him eating any mints and she didn't think he was the kind of man who would wear *any* cologne, let alone something that smelled like peppermint.

After she'd settled into her seat, Chase reached over and pulled her chair closer, then turned the laptop so she could see the screen.

It was open to an email from TJ. She quickly scanned the short note.

Chase,
Things are calm at the moment. Milena and JT are doing good. Don't

tell anyone, but she's pregnant. We're beyond thrilled, and Milena wanted me to make sure Sadie knows.

We haven't seen or heard from Jonathan, but I've been keeping a careful eye out since the FBI received that tip that he'd been spotted in the area. I appreciate you getting your commanding officer and the post general involved in what happened at the school...I've been officially cleared of any consequences for killing Jeremiah.

Oh...and please tell Sadie thank you from me again. She didn't have to stay once the school was shut down. She's a good woman and is always welcome in our home. She's tough as hell and I'm glad Milena has a friend like her.

~TJ

PS: Tell Sadie that Milena wants her to stand up with her at our wedding. No date yet, but as soon as Jonathan is caught, she should be prepared to come back down here because I'm not waiting a second longer than I have to in order to make Milena officially mine.

Sadie swallowed hard to try to keep the tears at bay. She'd only done what Milena would've done for *her* if the situation had been reversed. "Did you reply?" she asked Chase, trying to keep her voice normal. She wasn't like this. She didn't fall apart.

He eyed her for a long moment, but finally nodded. "Yeah. Told him you said hello and were worried about Milena. Also told him I agreed you're tough, but that I was pissed I didn't get to you before Jonathan'd had a chance to touch you."

"I'm no tougher than anyone else would've been in the same situation. I just did what needed to be done." She reached for her sandwich and opened her mouth to take a bite. Her eyes strayed to Chase—and she halted mid-bite at the look on his face. "What?"

"When you wouldn't tell me what happened in that room, I made inquiries on my own."

Sadie paled, but refused to rise to Chase's bait. He might be bluffing. He might not know what she'd done. But his next words dashed her hopes.

"You gave a complete statement to the Feds. I pulled some strings and got a copy."

"You had no right," Sadie said, looking down at her sandwich rather than at the man next to her. She'd never wanted anyone to know everything that had happened between her and Jonathan.

Something occurred to her then. She whipped her head up and stared at Chase in a panic. "You didn't tell my uncle or TJ, did you?" Only the Feds knew what she'd gone through during her hours trapped alone with Jonathan Jones. And she'd meant for it to stay that way.

But not even the Feds knew *everything*.

"No, Sparky, I didn't tell anyone." He reached out and turned her chin so she had no choice but to look him in the eyes. "Why? Why'd you do it? You could've gotten away. You had the chance."

"There was no way I was going to leave Milena at the school with Jonathan and his father. What kind of person would I be if I left her to suffer the consequences of my escape?"

Chase ran a hand over her hair and left his warm palm resting on the side of her neck. "Tell me what happened," he ordered.

"You already know," she protested.

"Tell me anyway."

Sadie struggled with herself. She wanted to put it all behind her, but how could she when Jonathan was still looking for her? When she was living in someone else's apartment and being guarded for her own protection? She wouldn't be able to put it behind her until she knew for sure that Jonathan wasn't ever going to pop out from behind a tree and force her to do everything he'd threatened.

"I woke up from whatever drug Jonathan had knocked us out with and saw Milena next to me, still unconscious. He'd untied us, so I got up, falling a couple of times before I got my balance back, and wandered over to a window. I realized we were at the school and tried to come up with a plan to get us out. I probably could've gotten out the window and disappeared into the night, but I couldn't leave Milena there by herself. Then I heard Jonathan and his father talking nearby." Sadie shuddered, hating the memory of how helpless she'd felt.

"They were talking about how Jeremiah was going to take Milena's son down to Mexico and start a new school, right?" Chase asked.

Sadie nodded. "Yeah. Then Jeremiah asked Jonathan if he thought he'd be able to 'get it up' long enough to impregnate me. Jonathan told his dad that he'd lifted my shirt and looked at my boobs, and while they were way too big, he could close his eyes and picture the babies I'd give him, and that would ensure he'd be able to get hard."

Taking a deep breath, Sadie closed her eyes, trying to control the nausea that nearly overwhelmed her at the thought of Jonathan Jones looking at her body when she'd been unconscious. Out of everything he'd done, that alone had the power to break her.

Well, that, and what he'd told her when he was handcuffing her to the bed in one of the rooms at the school.

"You're perfect," Chase said softly.

Sadie's eyes popped open and she stared at Chase.

"You're not too big. Your tits are perfect."

She wasn't sure how to respond for a moment, but humor finally won out. Sadie rolled her eyes and chuckled before responding. "Thanks. I think."

They shared a smile before Chase said, "Go on. What else?"

Sadie sighed. She'd tell him only what she'd told the Feds, leaving out the things she'd never told anyone—and swore she never would. "Jeremiah said he'd reconsider making Jonathan go to Mexico with him, if he would agree to give him one of my babies at some point down the line. They got into an argument about it, a loud one, and Jonathan threatened to hurt Milena. So I made sure they knew I was awake by pounding on the door. That distracted them, and Jonathan came in and hauled me out of the room. That's it. That's all I did."

"That's it?" Chase said, incredulously. "You could've snuck out of there while they were arguing. But you didn't. You stayed. And you obviously antagonized Jonathan until he decided, instead of disappearing with you immediately, he'd take the time to try to rape you right then and there! You shouldn't have antagonized him, Sparky. That wasn't smart."

"I know, I know. He got sick of me struggling and mouthing off and tied me up again. I guess he was waiting for his dad to finish doing whatever he was doing with Milena. He...he knocked me out and...when I woke up, he had fun trying to scare me by telling me what my future was going to be like. Then he dragged me into a room, where his father had Milena and JT. They said goodbye to one another, and...Jonathan took me into that room, the one you found me running out of. If you think you're an expert, what should I have done differently, Chase?"

Chase eyed her for a long moment. She tried not to feel guilty about the stuff she'd left out of her narrative, but she didn't want to think about what she'd done. She certainly didn't want to tell Chase. She kept her gaze on him, letting him see she really did want to know what he thought she should've done.

When he didn't answer immediately, she asked, "Chase?"

His lips were pressed together in a grim line, and he finally shook his head. "I don't know."

His answer shocked Sadie. She thought for sure he was going to tell her she should've run, or tried to hide, or tried to find a weapon...something.

He continued. "If I had been in your situation, I probably would've done the same thing. Especially when it came to keeping JT safe. I don't like that you had to put yourself in danger though. And I hope to Christ you aren't ever in that kind of situation again."

"Because I'm a woman?" Sadie knew what Chase's thoughts were on women in combat situations. He was opposed. They'd had this conversation before; it had irritated her then and it irritated her now.

"I know you don't understand or approve of my stance on this, Sparky," he began. "But will you let me tell you why I feel the way I do? And not interrupt me and try to change my mind this time?"

Sadie blushed. She *had* done that last time. Every time he'd begun to explain his thought process, she'd cut him off. It was juvenile of her and she regretted it. She wanted to know more about who he was as a person, including his principles. "Yeah."

"You know I'm in counterterrorism."

She nodded.

"And you know my sister was caught in that coup over in Egypt a while ago, right?"

Sadie nodded again.

"Right. I was deployed overseas not long after that. I had asked to be attached to a Special Forces unit, a team of Delta Force men. I wanted to understand Ghost a little better since it's obvious we're eventually going to be related to each other. The team I was imbedded with was given intel on the whereabouts of a kidnapped soldier. She was a truck driver. Had been minding her own business. Not in a combat position at all. But because she was a woman, the convoy was singled out. They killed the men with her and kidnapped her. The Delta Force team got intel on where she was being held and off we went."

Sadie got a sick feeling in her chest about where the story was headed. She put her hand on Chase's thigh in support. He covered it with his own and kept talking as if he didn't realize what he'd done.

"Everyone knows that America doesn't rest until they do all they can to get their MIA soldiers back. The enemy was counting on that. They purposely allowed the leak about the woman's location, then they laid in wait. We headed out, and before we could get anywhere close to the coordinates, the Humvees we were in were blown to pieces. The terrorists didn't even wait around to make sure we were dead. There were body parts and blood everywhere. Men I'd gotten to know and respect, gone, just like that."

He snapped his fingers, making Sadie jump in her seat at the sound.

"As far as I could see, there was only one man left alive besides me. But I didn't think there was any way he could survive. He was trapped under one of the vehicles and bleeding badly. I certainly wasn't in any shape to help him. I passed out, and when I came to, the man was gone. I guess the terrorists came back and found him and took him captive. I have no idea what happened to him because, since I wasn't officially in the unit, I didn't have the clearance to be informed. I tried to look him up in the Army system when I got back, but I don't have the clearance."

"But you're an officer, right?" Sadie protested, her heart breaking.

"Yeah, but that doesn't automatically mean I'd get information, even if I was working with the team, especially since he was Delta Force."

"How'd you get out of there?" Sadie asked, tightening her hand on his leg.

"Eventually another Army unit passed by, saw the carnage and found me."

"Does your sister know?"

"No one does. I haven't told anyone about it. Just you. Rayne knows I was injured, but I didn't let her know how close I'd come to being dead. Anyway, my point is that I have no problem with women being in the military. In a lot of ways, I think they make better soldiers than men. They're more level headed and cautious, which can be a good thing when you're dealing with volatile situations."

"But?" Sadie asked.

"These are *my* thoughts," Chase said. "Not the official Army stance. First, there's a matter of physical ability. There are some jobs, combat positions included, that just aren't physically suited to women. Not because of something they've done or not done, but because of body makeup. Some women could come to harm simply because of the physical requirements. But it's more than that. The threat of being abused by the enemy is always an issue." He held up a hand to forestall the argument he knew was coming. "I realize that both male and female soldiers are at risk of torture and rape, but the fact is, misogynistic terrorists may be more willing to abuse female prisoners. It's not the woman's fault, I'm not saying that at all, but the possibility is very real. It happened to my own sister when she was taken captive in Egypt. And it happened with that truck driver the Delta unit was trying to rescue."

Sadie didn't know how to respond. She was honestly floored. She'd met some amazing warriors when she was working at McKay-Taggart. And she knew they'd argue until their dying days for their right to defend their country in the same way men did. She understood that for someone like Chase, the thought of a woman being abused, his sister or otherwise, had to be a form of torture itself, but she was still struggling with his views. But she could admit that the more honorable the man, the more abhorrent the kind of situation he described would seem.

As if he could read her mind, Chase said, "I'm a traditional kind of man. I can't help it. I've had women superior officers and I respected the hell out of them. But if I went into combat with one of them... I know myself. I'd constantly be checking to ensure she wasn't in the line of fire and I'd do whatever was necessary to make sure she didn't fall into the hands of the enemy."

"But don't you think she'd do the same for you?" Sadie asked. "I know I'd do anything I could to help any one of my uncles, or the men and women who work at McKay-Taggart, if we were in a volatile situation."

"I know you would. But how effective do you think your uncle would be if he was constantly worried about *you* getting hurt?

"But what about *me*?" she asked again, trying to turn the argument around. "If I was in a situation where Sean, or Ian, or anyone from McKay-Taggart, was in danger, don't you think I'd be worried about them getting hurt too? You're looking at this the wrong way, Chase. I know you're protective, and I actually like that about you, but if the only thing between you and certain death was a woman, wouldn't you want her there to help you? To allow you to get home to your sister and those you loved? And you know what? *Men* can be raped if they were taken captive too. It would be just as horrifying for them as it would be for a woman. Maybe even *more* so because men don't normally worry about that sort of thing in their everyday life."

Sadie knew Chase's beliefs came from a position of concern for the opposite sex, not because he felt superior or wanted power and control over women. He hadn't complained about her little pink pistol in her purse that she carried everywhere. Hadn't bitched that she wanted to be kept up to date with information about Jonathan and his whereabouts. But she still thought he was wrong.

"Jonathan could've done that with you," Chase said, not addressing what she'd said. "If things turned out differently, he could've used you as a bargaining chip because he knew without a doubt that we wouldn't do anything that would potentially get you hurt. So, if you had to do that day you were kidnapped all over again? I have absolutely no idea what you could've done differently. I hate that you were in danger, and it makes me insane to think of you strapped to that bed, at his mercy. The outcome of that day could've been different if you hadn't done what you did. If you hadn't been there to distract Jonathan while Jeremiah was dealing with Milena and JT. But fuck if I ever want you to have to do something like that again."

"I don't want to be in that kind of situation again, either, Chase, but again, if Jonathan took *you* hostage, I wouldn't have done anything that would get you hurt either. It's not a matter of gender. It's a matter of being smart and using learned skills to get out of the situation."

Chase didn't agree, but he didn't disagree either. "At least think about it," she said.

"You're pretty good at this debate thing," Chase said with a smile.

"Did a semester on the debate team in college," she told him. Deciding to call a truce of sorts, Sadie didn't push the issue. She wasn't going to drop it, but she'd give him some time to think about what she'd said. She didn't like when they disagreed. As much as she had no problem sticking up for her beliefs, she preferred when she and Chase got along. He was funny, smart, and when he turned on the charm, she could forget she was basically living with him because she was in danger.

She liked Chase Jackson. He was honorable and he reminded her a lot of her uncles…but not in the familial sense. Chase could cook, he wasn't a slob, had a great work ethic, and was close to his sister. All good things in her book.

The bottom line was that if she wasn't hiding from Jonathan and whatever crazy thing he wanted to do to her, she'd be thrilled to be spending time with Chase and his friends. Maybe she would even try to find a way to act on her crazy attraction to the Army captain. He obviously felt the same. It wasn't exactly the time or the place, but if nothing else, her family had taught her to go for what she wanted. And what she wanted was to see if the sexual attraction between her and Chase was as explosive as it seemed.

She opened her mouth to change the subject to something less tense, and more flirtatious, when there was a knock at the door.

Chapter Four

When Sadie went to stand up, Chase stopped her with a hand on her shoulder. "Stay put. I'll get it."

He waited until she nodded, then headed for the door. Chase couldn't believe he'd told her about the incident overseas. He still hadn't recovered from it; knew he was a different man as a result. He also knew a lot of competent female soldiers who would kick his ass if they suspected he didn't want them anywhere near a combat zone, but he couldn't stop thinking about how easily they could be tortured and abused if they were captured, and the lengths to which men like the dead Delta Force team would go to rescue them.

But he also heard what Sadie was saying. He knew the reputation of the operatives at McKay-Taggart. The women were just as impressive as the men and he knew they would, and had, gone to the same lengths as the Delta Force teams he'd been imbedded with to rescue fellow soldiers and civilians alike.

Running a hand through his hair, he knew at some point he was going to have to tell Sadie she was right. Women were more than capable of kicking ass, and just as likely to go out of their way to protect the men they were serving with. It was a new way of thinking for him, but Chase was willing to be open minded if it meant getting closer to Sadie.

He looked through the peephole and blinked at who he saw on the other side of the door. He'd expected Fletch, or maybe even his sister, but he should've known he'd be seeing this visitor sooner or later.

Chase straightened and instead of immediately opening the door, gestured to Sadie. "You need to experience this for yourself."

Perplexed, she stood up and practically ran to his side. Chase opened the door with a flourish and smirked when Sadie's mouth fell open.

"Hi!" Fletch's little girl said brightly when she saw them. "I'm Annie. I live next door. Fletch is my daddy. I wanted to come over and see if you were using your TV."

"Uh…" Sadie looked at Chase.

He took pity on her and kneeled down so he was at eye level with Annie. "You remember me, right, squirt? Rayne is my sister."

Her eyes got huge. "Oh yeah! Are you younger or older?"

"Younger."

"Did you like having an older sister?"

"Yup."

"I want a little brother. Like, *bad*, but Mommy says I have to have paycents. But I want him *now* so I can play with him. Mommy's got a baby in her belly, but we don't know if I'm having a brother or a sister."

Chase swallowed his laughter. Annie was so earnest. He didn't have the heart to tell her that by the time Emily had the baby, when he or she was old enough to want to play, she'd probably want nothing to do with him, as she'd be in her teens. "It'll be a nice surprise either way," he told the little girl.

"I guess. Now…are you using your TV?"

Chase looked up at Sadie. "Are we using the TV?"

"Uh…no. We were just finishing up lunch."

"Cool." And with that, Annie walked by Chase and went straight to the little living room. She picked up the remote control from the coffee table, clicked on the TV, and surfed through a few channels before settling on an episode of the *Power Rangers*. She climbed onto the couch, pulled her knees up to her chest, and lost herself in the cartoon.

"Well, all right then," Sadie said, staring after the little girl. "Should we call her parents and let them know she's over here?"

Chase shut the door then turned to face her. "No need. They're aware she's here."

"How do you know?"

"Because if that was *my* little girl, I'd know every step she took outside my house. There's no way I'd let her wander around otherwise. Besides, Fletch has cameras all over this property."

"Oh, yeah. I remember you saying that."

"Right. I was going to suggest earlier that we call my sister and see if she wants to join us on a short shopping trip. I know your aunt packed more stuff for you, but I'm thinking you wouldn't mind going shopping anyway. And I'm fairly certain you wouldn't like shopping with me, because I don't shop, not in person. I buy everything I need online. But since Annie is here for who knows how long—and I'm not about to interrupt Fletch to ask him, because I'm guessing he's taking advantage of his daughter being out of the house and is otherwise preoccupied, which is exactly what I'd do in his shoes—how about we hang out, watch the *Power Rangers*, and when Annie leaves, I call my sister?"

Sadie looked up at him in shock. "You want to go shopping? With me? I thought we had to stay under the radar so Jonathan couldn't find me?"

"When I said we're going shopping, I didn't mean we're gonna skip around Temple, opening ourselves up to whatever Jonathan might want to lob our way. I know you hate to be confined, and the last month hasn't exactly been a walk in the park. I'm trying to kill two birds with one stone here…let you get out of the house for a bit while at the same time making sure I have your back. Unless you want to talk, that is. We can talk about whatever you left out of your recounting of what happened between you and Jonathan…" He let his words trail off.

"Shopping sounds great," Sadie exclaimed in a fake cheerful tone.

At her reaction, he had his confirmation that she really *had* left something out. He hated that, but wasn't going to pressure her…yet. "That's what I thought." He lowered his voice. "I don't mind if you don't want to talk about it…but that doesn't mean I'm going to stop trying to find out. And you should know, I was serious earlier, Sparky. You're mine."

At the shocked look on her face, Chase hoped she understood what he meant. He didn't want or need a Dominant/submissive relationship, but he did want to care for Sadie. To make sure she had everything she needed and wanted, both in and out of the bedroom. That was what her being "his" meant to him. And part of that also meant finding out what she'd hidden from him earlier.

He could tell from her facial expressions and nonverbal cues that she'd left something out in her recounting of her time spent with Jonathan. He hadn't pushed, hoping the greater the time since the events in San Antonio, and the longer she was around him, the safer she'd feel. But it was obvious that whatever had happened between her and Jonathan Jones was still haunting her. And he wanted to know what it was, but he wanted her to *want* to tell him. To trust him with it.

"Have you ever seen a *Power Rangers* cartoon before?" Sadie asked, looking back at the television. "It's super violent, but there's always a good message in there too."

"Mmmm," Chase murmured, letting her change the subject.

Chase took her hand and marveled anew at the feel of it in his own. He pulled her over to the couch and sat her down. "I'll put the plates away. Stay," he ordered when she went to stand back up.

Forty-five minutes later, there was another knock on the door.

"I got it," Chase said softly, motioning for Sadie to continue sitting. Even though he was fairly sure it was one of Annie's parents on the other side, he still wouldn't let Sadie get up. One, she was still in danger, but two, it just wasn't gentlemanly.

His dad had drilled it into him that there were just some things that men did, and one of those things was, when your woman was half asleep on the couch with a seven-year-old child snuggled in her lap, you do *not* make her get up to get the door, fetch you a beer, or make you supper.

He missed his parents. They'd died too early in a freak plane accident while on a cruise to Alaska, but he hadn't realized until right this second the deeper implications of what their absence meant. They'd never meet the woman he married. They'd never meet his children, their grandchildren. And he'd never get to tell his father that he'd been absolutely right when he'd told him all those years ago that when he met the woman he wanted to make his own, he'd know it immediately.

Chase silently stalked to the door of the apartment and looked through the peephole. Fletch. He opened the door with a smile.

"Hey."

"Jackson," Fletch said with a slight grin. "You don't happen to have my little sprite over here, do you?"

"You know I do," Chase said, stepping away from the door.

Fletch lowered his voice. "Sorry, man. Couldn't resist the chance to have my wife to myself for a while."

"Figured as much. She's watching *Power Rangers* with Sadie." Chase turned to head back into the small living area, but Fletch stopped him with a hand on his shoulder.

He motioned to the living room. "How's she doing?"

Chase shook his head and lowered his voice. "On the outside, fine. But I think there's something she's still not talking about that happened when she and Jonathan were alone in that school. We know he wanted to get her pregnant. But other than the five minutes or so before her rescue, when he tried to handcuff her to a bed—which is part of the official report—she's really skittish about discussing the rest of the time she spent alone with him. Says he knocked her out a second time."

Fletch opened his mouth as if he was going to speak, then shut it again.

"What?"

"I was just going to say, whatever it is, go easy, man. She acts like she can take on the world single-handedly, but underneath that bluster and strength is one scared-as-hell woman."

"You think I don't know that?" Chase asked.

"I'm gonna say something else here, and I hope you don't take it the wrong way. I don't know you that well, but I know you're Rayne's brother, and she'd do absolutely anything for you. *Anything*. Rayne's smart in a lot of ways, but she's also not experienced enough to see what me and the others see. Somethin's eatin' at you. Same as it's eatin' at Sadie. Not sure what it is or when it happened, but just like you know that Sadie needs to get something off her chest, you need to do the same."

"I'm fine," Chase said immediately.

Fletch held up a hand. "Yeah, that's what we all say, but it's complete and utter bullshit. I'm not sayin' you need to tell *me*. Or your sister. But you need to find someone you can unload that crap on. All of it. Not just the superficial stuff. One thing I've learned over the years being on the team is that if you don't lance the wound, it continues to fester."

The two men stared at each other without saying a word. Chase knew Fletch was right, but he wasn't quite ready to talk to anyone else about the Delta Force team that had been murdered yet. He wasn't sure why he'd told Sadie, except that it had felt right. The good men who were blown up right in front of his eyes. They had families…children. Why he'd survived when they hadn't… It hadn't made sense to him then and it didn't make sense to him even today.

He nodded once at Fletch. A brief movement of his head.

Fletch returned the nod and clapped Chase on the back. "Right, so…my monkey cause any problems?"

"Of course not. You have your hands full though," Chase told the other man.

"Yup. Wouldn't have it any other way."

"She informed us that she wants her little brother…like pronto."

Fletch chuckled. "Yeah, she tells us that every other day too. We keep telling her she has to be patient. That the baby inside Mommy's belly isn't done growing yet, but she doesn't seem to care much."

"Everything okay with Em?" Chase tried to ask delicately.

"She's good. The baby is progressing normally. And in the meantime, we're enjoying the hell out of her increased libido."

Chase chuckled. "I bet you are. But word of warning…"

"What's that?"

"I don't want to ever know anything about my sister and Ghost's love life. That's just TMI, you know?"

Fletch outright laughed. When he got himself under control, he said, "I'll let him know."

"Appreciate it."

"Daddddddy!"

Fletch had just enough time to turn and open his arms before a little bundle of messy hair and childlike exuberance threw herself into his arms. "Hey, sprite. Have a good time?"

She nodded against his shoulder. "Yeah! The Maze monster captured the Power Rangers, but Ryan was able to use his smarts instead of his guns and they gotted free. But then Fury was all like, *pew pew pew*, and the ranger shot back, *pew pew pew*, and the bad guys were all dead!"

Fletch shook his head. "We need to find you a new show, squirt."

Annie scrunched up her forehead and frowned up at him. "Why?"

"*Pew, pew, pew?*"

The little girl giggled.

Chase was grinning at the big bad Delta Force soldier snuggling with his little girl—until he turned his head and looked at Sadie.

Sadie was standing by the couch, arms crossed over her chest and a faraway look in her eyes. Chase's feet were moving before his brain gave them the command to do so.

He stood in front of her and asked in a soft tone, "Sadie?"

She jerked and her eyes swung up to his. "Yeah?"

"You okay?"

"Uh huh."

"What were you thinking just now?"

She shrugged, but said in a quiet voice, "Just about some of the kids at the school down in San Antonio."

Chase's eyes gentled, and he put a hand up and stroked the apple of her cheek with his thumb.

Her head bobbed a fraction of an inch. "They were so innocent. Jeremiah and Jonathan really screwed them up. They brainwashed them into thinking what they were doing to them was normal. That sex between adults and kids was fine. I worry about where they are now, who they've living with, what they're thinking. They have to be so confused."

Chase wasn't sure what to say to make her feel better.

Fletch's voice sounded from behind Chase. "With counseling, hopefully they'll be okay, Sadie."

She nodded but didn't look convinced.

"Put me down, Daddy," Annie said softly.

Fletch leaned over and placed Annie on her feet. The little girl immediately went over to where Sadie was standing and wrapped her arms around her waist. She laid her head on Sadie's belly and simply held her.

Chase watched as Sadie's surprised gaze went from him, to Fletch, and finally down to Annie. He saw the moment she lost the iron control she'd been holding on to. Her arms went around Annie and her head drooped. Chase took a step toward the two and put one hand on Annie's head and the other on the side of Sadie's neck. They stood like that for several moments before Annie lifted her head and looked up to the woman she had her arms around.

"Feel better?"

Sadie gave her a wobbly smile. "Yeah, thanks, Annie. Your hug is amazing."

"I know," Annie said, as if she knew her arms held magical powers and it was no big thing. "Wanna see my Army man? I used to have two, but my boyfriend has the other one. He lives out in California and we're gonna get married someday."

"What?"

Fletch broke in before Annie could explain. "Not now, squirt. Sadie and Jackson have stuff they need to do."

"What stuff?" Annie asked, looking up at Sadie.

Sadie had no idea, so she turned her gaze to Chase in question.

"We're meeting with Rayne later."

"Oooooh, I haven't seen Rayne in forever!" Annie gushed. "Can I come too? Please, please, please, please?"

"You saw her two days ago, Annie. And no, you can't go with Chase and Sadie. We're going to go to Fort Hood and check out that new obstacle course…remember?"

Without a word, Annie spun away from Sadie and raced for the front door. She wrenched it open and was gone.

Fletch chuckled. "Knew that would light a fire under her butt. The kid loves obstacle courses like a squirrel loves nuts."

Chase grinned.

"Anyway, thanks for keeping your eye on Annie this morning. Most of the team is gone, but I thought I'd invite Ghost and Rayne over since they're around and we could have a small barbeque tonight at the house. You want to come over?"

Chase turned to Sadie. "Since Fletch has the biggest place, he usually hosts their get-togethers."

"You want me to come?" Sadie asked hesitantly.

"Why wouldn't I?" Fletch asked.

"Well…because Jonathan wants to find me, kidnap me, probably rape and kill me, and he won't care who gets in his way to do it? Your wife and kid will be there, right? It might put them in danger."

Before Fletch could answer, Chase stepped into Sadie's personal space and backed her against a wall. His hands went to her waist and he held her tightly as he said, "No one is going to kidnap you, Sparky. Fletch's yard and house is probably the safest place you could be… The cameras are all connected to Fletch's watch, so he'll know the second someone steps foot on his property. Besides, I'll be here too. I'll keep you safe."

"If you're sure… The last thing I want to do is drag someone else, especially another child, into this fucked-up situation. It was bad enough Jonathan and his father hurt those girls at Bexar, but then they brought JT into things—"

"Annie will be safe," Fletch interrupted. "I know you haven't been around her other than this morning, but she knows how to take care of herself…more than I'd like, actually. It's just a barbeque, Sadie. A few men and their women hanging out, drinking beers and eating some good food. Don't overthink it."

"In that case, I'd love to," Sadie said. Her gaze went from Fletch to Chase, who was still standing in her personal space.

"Great. I'll see you later then. Around five?" Fletch asked Chase.

"Sounds good."

After Fletch left, Sadie looked at Chase. "Wanna let me go so I can get ready for shopping?"

Did he want to let her go? No, actually, he didn't. "No."

She looked surprised for a moment, then annoyance crept in. "Chase, step back."

Instead of doing what she asked, he stepped forward until his thighs touched hers. He slid a hand around to the small of her back and pulled her into him until her breasts brushed against his chest.

She looked at him with her eyes wide with shock and her brows drawn in confusion. Her hands came up and gripped his T-shirt on either side of his waist. "Chase—"

"Jonathan isn't going to touch you. Tell me you believe that," he ordered.

Sadie pushed at him for a moment, but when he didn't loosen his grip, she merely sighed. "Fine. I believe you."

He brought one hand up to her face and tilted her chin so she had no choice but to look him in the eyes. "Now say it like you mean it."

"You're just like some of the guys at McKay-Taggart," Sadie told him. "All macho dominant, sure that you're Superman and nothing can touch you. News flash—you can't promise that. Shit happens, I've seen it firsthand. People get hurt. They disappear. Chase, you don't know Jonathan. You don't know what he's like. If he wants to get his hands on me, he will. You can't guard me all day, every day. Eventually, I'll have to go back up to Dallas. To my job, to my life. He'll just wait me out. Postpone the inevitable until you aren't around."

Chase wanted to immediately rebuff her words, but he took a moment to examine the woman in his arms before he replied. Her hands were gripping his shirt as if he were the only thing holding her together. Her lips were pressed together in a thin line, and he could see the pulse hammering in her throat. She wasn't mad, she was fucking terrified.

"Tell me what happened inside that room, Sparky," he ordered gently.

Sadie shook her head.

"Please?"

Her eyes dropped down and to the right, but Chase didn't release her chin. Finally, her eyes came back to his. "I don't want you to think badly of me."

"Sadie, I absolutely am not going to think badly about you for anything you may or may not have done while inside that hellhole."

"I think badly about myself."

Chase's stomach clenched. He hated that. Abhorred it. "You have absolutely no reason to think that way."

"I do," she told him.

Chase looked at her for a long moment, then said, "How about we table this conversation until tonight?"

The relief on her face was easy to read. "Yes."

"We'll go shopping with Rayne. Have dinner with Fletch and Ghost. Then tonight when we're back here, relaxed after a couple of beers, we'll talk. It'll be easier."

"It's not going to be easier," Sadie told him.

"It will. Trust me. Talking about what's fucking with your mind is a lot easier in the dark than the light of day."

Sadie's eyes whipped up to his. She peered at him intensely for a beat before whispering, "Okay."

"Okay." Then Chase pulled the woman who had stolen his heart into his embrace. She buried her face into his shoulder and they stood like that for a minute or two. Simply enjoying being held by each other.

"I need to call Rayne," Chase said, pulling away.

"Okay."

"I'm not sure how long it will take her to get over here."

"Can I go lie down until she arrives?" Sadie asked.

"Of course. Take a nap. I'll wake you up when it's time to go."

Without another word, Sadie took a step to the side and headed toward the bedroom.

Chase ran his hand through his hair. Sean Taggart had asked him to keep him informed regarding anything he found out from Sadie about what had happened to her. Her uncle knew as well as he did that something had to have transpired between his niece and Jeremiah's son. He wouldn't be so hell-bent on getting to her if it hadn't. Whatever it was had Sadie completely torn up inside.

He'd have to wait until she told him to decide what, if anything, he'd relay to her uncle. The man was lethal. He could be sweet with Sadie and his wife, but Chase knew without a doubt, he'd kill Jonathan if the situation warranted it. Hell, any of the Taggarts would.

But they'd have to get in line behind *him*. He needed to know what happened between Sadie and Jonathan, what she wasn't telling him—but he also didn't want to know. He *did* know, however, without a doubt, that tonight would change his and Sadie's relationship. He hoped it brought them closer together, but he also knew, after hearing whatever it was she was so ashamed of, it could drive them apart.

Because if she told him Jonathan had violated her…had taken her against her will… Chase knew without a doubt that he'd tell the Taggarts he couldn't look after their niece anymore—so he could go AWOL and hunt down that son of a bitch and kill him with his bare hands.

Chapter Five

Sadie hadn't been sure what Chase's sister would think of her, but she shouldn't have worried. Rayne Jackson took one look at her and immediately gave her a big hug.

"I'm so sorry you were caught in the middle of that situation, Sadie. How awful. Are you okay? Were you hurt? I also can't believe you've been at my brother's apartment for a month and he didn't tell me! Is he taking care of you? I love him, but he's a guy... Sometimes he has no clue about what women need."

Sadie stepped back, right into Chase. He put a hand on her waist to steady her. She turned her head to thank him and saw he was grinning at his sister.

"What do you mean I don't know what women need? When you were eight and had the chicken pox, I brought you a whole cup of worms to make you feel better."

Sadie shared a look with Rayne and giggled when she rolled her eyes.

"Or the time when you were upset over some boy when we were in middle school, and to help, I got into your Myspace account and posted that picture of you asleep in your bed with chicken pox scabs all over your face and asked that everyone send you good wishes."

"You didn't," Sadie asked Chase with big eyes.

He grinned and shrugged. "I was helping."

"See?" Rayne asked Sadie. "He has no clue."

"What about the time Ghost came to me after he rescued you from that coup in Egypt and I didn't beat the shit out of him when he said that you were 'his'? Or when I gave you that barrette that ended up helping to save your life? Or when we had that long talk because you were upset about Ghost being away on a mission and you came to *me* and I let you eat my entire pint of double chocolate brownie ice cream I had in my freezer?"

Sadie watched the irritation melt off Rayne's face. "Yeah, all right, sometimes you know exactly what women need." She turned back to Sadie. "I just want you to know if you need someone to talk to, I'm here."

"But you don't even know me," Sadie blurted before she could think about what she was saying.

"Hopefully after today, I'll know you better. Besides, I heard all about what happened down at that school from Ghost. You and your friend… What was her name?"

"Milena," Sadie said.

"Right. From what I hear, you and your friend Milena were amazingly calm and helped make sure the head guy wasn't able to get away and abuse hundreds of other girls."

"That's not exactly—"

Rayne held up her hand. "Whatever. The point is, anyone who can hold her own against fake teachers and philanthropists who are actually pedophiles is someone I want to be friends with. So, after today, if there's anything you need, just let me know and I'll make sure you get it. Snacks, time away from my annoying little brother, clothes, a friend to drink with… I've got your back."

"Wow. Uh…thanks."

"You're welcome."

"Can I ask something?"

"Sure," Rayne said breezily.

"Chase gave you a barrette that helped save your life…?"

Rayne smiled at her brother, the love in her eyes clear to see. Sadie didn't have any brothers or sisters, but she knew without a doubt, no matter how much they might tease, Rayne and Chase would do anything for each other.

"Long story, one I'm sure Chase will be happy to tell you," Rayne said softly.

"Speaking of which," Chase said. "I've got a new prototype…a bracelet that comes apart and has a hidden blade inside. You want it?"

"Duh, of course I do," Rayne told her brother.

"I'll get it to Ghost as soon as I can."

"Awesome. You guys ready to go?" Rayne asked, changing the subject and motioning toward the door. "I stopped over and saw Emily and Annie before I came up here, and Fletch informed me that I'm coming over for a barbeque tonight. Good timing, because I have an overnight flight that leaves tomorrow."

"Overnight flight?" Sadie asked as she turned to pick up her purse from the kitchen table.

"Yeah, I'm a flight attendant. I used to work the international routes, but after the Egypt thing, I really wasn't interested in that much anymore. So now I work the shorter domestic flights. I'm headed to Los Angeles tomorrow, will spend the night, then come back the next day."

"Do you have those a lot?" Sadie asked.

Rayne shrugged. "Enough that Ghost gets grumpy when I'm gone too long. But honestly, I prefer the day trips because I've found that I don't sleep well by myself anymore." She smiled, apparently not at all shy about sharing. "There's just something relaxing and calming about falling asleep in Ghost's arms and waking up the same way."

Chase held up his hands. "Gettin' too close to too much information there, sis."

"Whatever. TMI would actually be if I'd said that we both like to sleep naked so when I wake up horny, we don't have to take the time to pull off our clothes. Ghost can just rip the covers off and—"

Rayne stopped speaking and laughed when Chase put both hands over his ears and began to hum so he couldn't hear what she was saying.

Rayne turned to Sadie. "He's so easy to tease."

Sadie tried not to laugh, she really did, but Chase looked so miserable, she couldn't help it. She'd seen Chase in action; he was one tough, scary guy. But at the moment, he looked like he wanted to throw up at the mere mention of his sister's sex life.

"Not fair that you guys are ganging up on me," he pouted after he'd lowered his hands. "Seriously, sis. Not cool. You know I don't want to hear about your sex life."

"Tough. It's payback for all those times you made my life miserable when we were growing up."

"Come on, let's get this over with," Chase said grumpily. "Too much sister time is bad for my health."

Rayne merely laughed and hooked her arm with Chase's. "You love me, you know it."

"I do. But if you don't stop torturing me by talking about your sex life, I'm going to have to do something drastic."

"Like what?" she taunted.

They waited while Chase locked the apartment door and then they all headed down the stairs, Rayne in front, Chase following her, and Sadie bringing up the rear.

"Turnabout is fair play. You want to know about *my* sex life? What my favorite positions are, how I like to be touched, and how good my woman feels when I'm inside her?"

Sadie would've fallen down the stairs if Chase hadn't been in front of her. Hearing him talk about sex so casually, to his sister no less, made her heart skip a beat.

Chase caught her easily, keeping her upright. His eyes met hers as he added, "How every time I look at her, I want to tear her clothes off and make her scream for me?"

Sadie held her breath. Oh my God. Was he talking to *her* or his sister?

"Ewwww," Rayne said, continuing to move down the stairs, not even noticing that Chase had stopped. "Gross! Okay, you're right. I have no desire to think about you without any clothes on. It was bad enough I saw everything you had when you were ten and I accidentally walked in on you in the bathroom. I'll stop teasing you about me and Ghost. Ick!"

"Chase," Sadie whispered. "We need to go."

"I do, you know," he said softly, ignoring her warning.

She tried to hold back the question, but couldn't. "Do what?"

His eyes roamed from the top of her head down to her chest, then back up before his nostrils flared and he took a deep breath. "Never mind," he muttered. Then leaned close, kissed her forehead before making sure she was steady on her feet again, and continued down the stairs.

Sadie stood stock-still for a heartbeat. She could feel the warmth of his lips on her forehead even though he was no longer touching her. She'd seen her uncle kiss her aunt like that countless times. It was an affectionate gesture. One that had always touched something deep inside her. That easy affection between them was somehow much more intimate than if they'd publically shared a tongue-curling, passionate kiss. It was something they did when they were around their kids, or Sadie, that showed how much they loved each other.

And Chase had just kissed her the same way.

She was so screwed.

Sadie knew, at that moment, that she wanted Chase. For as long as he'd have her. One night, two. It didn't matter that they disagreed about stuff all the time. It didn't matter that she was only supposed to be staying with him until Jonathan was caught. It didn't matter that it would tear her heart out when she left to go home to Dallas. She'd take what she could get, soak it all in, and try to pick up the pieces of her heart when he let her go.

"Coming?" Rayne called up to Sadie as she stood on the steps, frozen, as if Chase's lips had turned her to stone.

Sadie shook her head, trying to get herself back under control. "Yeah, I'm coming," she told Rayne, taking a deep breath and heading for Chase's car as if he hadn't shattered her with a simple touch of his lips on her skin.

* * * *

It was after a trip to the Temple mall and a short stop to grab some alcohol for the get-together that night, and when they were coming back to the car after stopping at the grocery store to stock the little apartment with food, that it happened.

Sadie was laughing at something Rayne was saying when she felt Chase stiffen at her side. "Wha—"

She didn't get anything else out before Chase grabbed her arm and yanked, spinning her around until she was behind him. He shoved her hard enough that she went flying toward a parked SUV. Luckily, she put out her hands and caught herself, otherwise her face would've smashed into the glass on the driver's side door.

She turned and saw Chase hustling his sister toward her in the same urgent, not-gentle-at-all way. It would've been comical—Rayne still had ahold of the grocery cart and Chase was literally dragging her *and* the cart to where he'd basically thrown Sadie—but because of the deadly look on Chase's face, it wasn't. She opened her mouth to ask what was going on, but Chase beat her to it.

"I saw someone crouched by my car. Stay here. Stay down. Do. Not. Move. I'll be right back."

And with that, he was gone.

"Shit," Sadie muttered, knowing whatever was happening couldn't be good.

Rayne dug into her purse and pulled out her cell phone. She pushed a couple of buttons and put the phone up to her ear.

"I'm in the parking lot of Walmart with my brother and Sadie. He just shoved us behind an SUV and told us he saw someone hanging around his car." She paused, listening to what whoever was on the other end of the line was saying. Then she said, "Right. Okay." Another pause. Then, "I don't know." Finally, after a long moment, she whispered, "I love you. Bye."

Sadie waited impatiently for Rayne to hang up. When she didn't say anything about their situation, Sadie whispered, "We need to do something to help Chase."

Rayne shook her head. "Ghost said to stay put."

Sadie ground her teeth in frustration and lifted her head enough so she could look through the window of the car they were hiding behind. She didn't see anything unusual, and Chase was nowhere in sight. She turned back to Rayne and gestured toward the phone she was still clenching in her fist. Her fingers were white with the tension of her grip. "Ghost is coming?"

Rayne nodded.

For some reason, Sadie was more freaked out now than she'd been back at the school when Jonathan had pushed her down on the bed. Maybe it was because she didn't know what was going on. Maybe it was because Chase could be in danger. She wasn't sure. But she *was* sure she didn't like the feeling. Not at all. She had no idea what had happened to the badass Sadie she'd been up in Dallas, but at the moment, she felt completely out of her league.

"Maybe we should go back into the store," she finally suggested.

"No," Rayne replied immediately. "Ghost said to stay put, so we're staying put."

She didn't want to say it out loud, but she was wondering what would happen if whoever it was that Chase saw circled around and came at them from behind.

Suddenly knowing the person Chase saw was Jonathan, Sadie began to shake. She knew Jonathan was obsessed. She also knew she'd tricked him, and he was beyond pissed about it.

But crouching by that SUV in the middle of the day, wondering if Chase was all right, Sadie knew without a doubt, after he'd had his way with her, Jonathan was going to kill her. She'd wounded his ego. His male pride. And with the way he'd been raised by Jeremiah, he wasn't going to just get over it. He'd need to prove that he was man enough to deal with her.

She didn't know how much time had passed, but it seemed to be going by extremely slowly. She wished she had her small pink gun on her, but she'd stupidly left it back in the apartment over the garage. Sadie wanted Ghost there *now*. Hell, anyone who could help Chase would be super. For the first time, she understood a bit better what the men and women of McKay-Taggart did on a daily basis. How in the world the wives, and husbands, dealt with knowing their spouses were facing bad guys like this was beyond her. She hated the thought of Chase being in danger. Especially since it was because of her.

When she couldn't take the waiting for another second, Sadie peered over the edge of the door once more, needing to see Chase. Needing to make sure he was all right.

As if her thoughts about Jonathan had conjured him out of thin air, she saw him crouched behind a car a row over from where Chase's vehicle was parked.

She knew it was Jonathan because he turned his head and looked right at her.

She'd recognize his blond hair, pointed nose, and the hateful look in his icy blue eyes anywhere. Even across a parking lot.

He turned from her then and aimed his pistol.

Sadie looked in the direction he was facing and saw Chase cautiously moving between two cars near Jonathan. Her mouth was open and she was yelling at Chase before she even thought about what she was doing.

"Chase! Behind you! He's behind that red car!"

He spun at the same time Jonathan pulled the trigger. The small-caliber pistol he held made a slight popping noise, which seemed somehow muffled in the busy public parking lot.

Her eyes glued to Chase, she held her breath until he took two giant steps and disappeared behind a Jeep. "Oh my God," she said softly. Her eyes went back to where Jonathan had been hiding behind the car, but he was gone.

"Where'd he go?" she said, more to herself than Rayne.

"There he is," Rayne said, pointing off to the side. "And Ghost is with him now."

Sadie looked where her new friend was pointing and saw Chase huddled with Ghost. She hadn't been asking about Chase, though. She'd been wondering where *Jonathan* had gone.

Before she could freak about it, Fletch materialized next to them.

"Come on," he said, motioning toward an idling Highlander SUV nearby.

"Did Ghost call you?" Rayne asked.

Fletch looked at her as if she were insane. "Yeah, Rayne, he did. Now come on, we need to get out of here."

"What about our groceries?" she asked. "It would suck to get Sadie all the way back home, only for her to realize she has to come back here to get something to eat."

"Jonathan was by a red car," Sadie told Fletch, ignoring Rayne's asinine argument about the food. "Chase didn't see him, and he got off a shot."

"Ghost has his back," Fletch reassured her.

Sadie looked around for Chase for a moment but no longer saw him. She turned to Fletch and nodded. "Okay."

"He's going to meet us at the house. I need to get you out of here, Sadie, in case Jonathan decides to go after you next."

"Are the cops coming?" Rayne asked.

"Doesn't look like it," Fletch told her. "No one seemed to notice the gunshot. He probably has a silencer on his gun."

"How's that even possible?" Sadie asked, shaking her head. "I heard it."

"You were looking right at him when he shot, right?" Fletch asked.

"Yeah."

"You heard it because you were watching him. Even with all the mass shootings happening lately, people don't expect something like that here in the middle of the day, in the middle of a Walmart parking lot. And even if they did hear it, they probably thought it was a car backfiring or something. Now come on, we have to get out of here."

Fletch quickly led them over to the black SUV with tinted windows. Sadie struggled, suddenly not wanting to leave without making sure Chase was all right.

"Sadie, get in," Fletch told her.

"I want to see Chase," Sadie told him, putting out a hand to brace herself so she couldn't be shoved into the backseat.

"He's fine. *Get in*," the man repeated.

"If Emily was shot at and you didn't know if she was hurt or not, would you leave her to continue on with a mission? Even if I told you she was okay and in the hands of another guy like yourself?"

"Yes," Fletch said immediately. "If she was with Chase or Ghost or any of my other friends, I'd trust them to get her the fuck away from the situation safely. Get in the damn car, Sadie."

It finally sank in that she was being ridiculous. Not only that, she was putting Chase and Ghost in danger by hesitating. Possibly Rayne, Fletch, and herself too. Her uncles would kick her ass if she did the same thing to them in the middle of a dangerous situation.

Without another word, she ducked her head and climbed into the backseat.

While she'd been trying to convince Fletch to let her see Chase, Rayne had grabbed their groceries and thrown them into the SUV. Crazy woman.

The second Fletch was behind the wheel, he peeled out of the parking lot as if the hounds of hell were after them.

Rayne put her hand on Sadie's leg in silent support as they sped through the city back to Fletch's house.

Chapter Six

"What the fuck, Jackson?" Ghost asked once the truck had disappeared and they'd searched the parking lot thoroughly. Somehow Jonathan had managed to slip away once more. "You okay?"

Chase winced and tried to ignore the throbbing in his arm. He'd heard Sadie's warning just in time and was able to avoid being hit in the chest. He'd thrown himself to the side, but not before being nailed in the arm instead of the heart. It hurt like a motherfucker, but that was much better than being dead.

"I'm good," he told Ghost. He'd bleed for a while, but with the way his arm felt, he knew the bullet hadn't torn through an artery or otherwise put him in a situation where he needed to go to the emergency room.

Ghost was professional enough not to second-guess him. He merely grunted and asked, "What happened?"

"We were headed to my car and I noticed someone lurking around it. I got the women stashed away and came over to check it out. All four tires are flat, and I haven't looked under the hood, but I'm guessing it probably won't start."

"And your arm?"

"Jonathan was hiding like the pansy chickenshit he is. From the sound of it, he was using an M&P. Sadie gave me enough of a head's up that he didn't put a bullet in my fucking chest."

"You sure it was him?"

"Yeah. I didn't get a good look, but that's what I'm assuming."

"You telling her uncle?" Ghost asked.

Chase nodded. "It's been a while since that second time he slipped away from the school, and we'd hoped the recent sighting of him was mistaken identity. That maybe this time, he really *had* gotten the fuck out of Texas. But it looks like our original fears about him coming after Sadie are true."

"What the fuck happened to make him so determined to get to her?"

That was the million-dollar question. And it had to be more than his sick plan to impregnate her so he could abuse his own children. That was bad enough... But the obsession Jonathan had for Sadie was extreme.

And Chase would be finding out tonight every detail about Sadie's time alone with him, no matter how reluctant she was to talk about it. He couldn't keep her safe if she didn't tell him what they were up against.

"I don't know," Chase admitted. "Sadie doesn't want to talk about it. Has barely admitted that something more happened than what she'd already told the Feds. Acts like she's ashamed."

Taking another look around, Ghost motioned toward his black Crown Victoria. They quickly walked toward the car. Once they were inside, Ghost started it up and headed out of the parking lot toward Fletch's place. "I don't give a shit what she did or said," Ghost growled in a low, deadly tone. "Those assholes were perverted and insane. They fucked up so many kids' lives. I don't know what happened that day Jonathan's father was killed, but I do know that Sadie has nothing to be ashamed of."

"Agreed."

"But here's the question," Ghost went on. "If she tells you that she slept with the man before you showed up...you gonna lose your shit?"

Chase opened his mouth—and nothing came out. He licked his lips then finally said, "I wasn't there. I didn't have to hear him talk about abusing little girls. I wasn't trying to keep my friend and her son safe until help showed up. Help she had no idea *was* going to show up. So no, if she tells me that she didn't fight as that asshole raped her, I'm not going to lose my shit. I'll continue to tell her that she has nothing to be ashamed of."

"You want her." It wasn't a question.

"I want her," Chase agreed immediately. "And she'll be mine. Fuck, she already feels like mine and we haven't even kissed yet. I've had some time to think about our relationship, and I can tell you unequivocally that I would do anything to have her by my side."

"Give up your Army career?" Ghost asked.

Chase huffed out a breath. "Wow, don't beat around the bush, Ghost. Go right for the jugular."

"I'll tell you this," Ghost said quietly. "If it was a matter of my career or Rayne, I'd choose your sister every time."

Chase knew that the man sitting next to him loved his sister. Hell, it was more than obvious. But Chase also knew how much Ghost loved the Army. Loved being a Delta Force member. For him to say he'd give it up was big. Huge.

But then he thought about Sadie. About giving her up and about the possibility of her loving another man, starting a family with him, and his stomach clenched. "Yeah," he said, conviction in every word. "I'd give up my career for her."

Ghost clamped him on the shoulder as they drove. "Welcome to being pussy whipped. I wouldn't change it for all the money in the world."

The men grinned at each other. Slowly, Chase's smile died. "I need to call Sean Taggart."

"Don't envy you, man," Ghost said.

Chase grimaced. "Might as well get it over with." He gently pulled his phone out of his pocket, being careful not to jostle his arm, and pressed a few buttons on the phone.

"Taggart."

"Sean. It's Chase Jackson."

"What's up?"

Chase took a deep breath and didn't beat around the bush, figuring Sean wouldn't appreciate it. "Looks like Jonathan is going to be a problem after all, and it's a good thing I'm looking after Sadie."

"What happened?" Sean's voice changed from the casual, laid-back tone he'd had just a moment ago to that of the no-nonsense, ready-to-take-action former Green Beret that he was.

"Shots fired in a public parking lot."

"Fuck. At Sadie?"

"No. Me. I got her out of the way when I saw someone lurking around my car. While I was tracking him down, the fucker took a shot at me. If it hadn't been for Sadie warning me, he might've succeeded in taking me out. He wants to get his hands on her. Bad."

"If one hair on her head is hurt, he's gonna wish he'd never fucked with a Taggart."

She wasn't a Taggart, but Chase knew what Sean meant. His wife was Sadie's mom's sister. And since Sean loved his wife more than anything, and Grace loved her niece, anyone who threatened Sadie, basically threatened his wife. And one thing Chase had learned from his research into the McKay-Taggart group, *no one* fucked with what was theirs. He was beginning to appreciate the sentiment.

"You catch the asshole?"

"No. Just like at the school, he disappeared like smoke."

"Where is Sadie now?"

"She's on her way to Fletch's house." Sean knew who Fletch was. He knew who all the Delta Force men were. He and his brother had researched everyone Sadie had any contact with down in San Antonio. He'd first found out as much as he could about TJ and Milena, and had learned TJ had done a favor for the Delta Force team in the past. And because Sean wasn't one to let loose strings hang, he'd gone on to research Ghost and the others on the team. If he had found anything he didn't like, Chase knew full well Sadie wouldn't still be with him. Sean would've forced her back up to Dallas no matter what she *or* Chase wanted.

"You're not with her?"

Not liking the accusation in Sean's tone, Chase said tersely, "No. She's with Fletch. He took her and Rayne back to the house so we could search the parking lot. Fucker clipped my arm. I wasn't sure if the cops were called or not, and didn't want her anywhere near here in case a report was made. Wanted to keep her out of it."

"Clipped?" Sean asked.

"Yeah."

There was silence on the other end of the line for a long moment. Just when Chase didn't think Sean was going to say anything else, or thought maybe he'd hung up, he said, "You like my niece."

Fuck. This again. But Chase would reassure whoever the fuck he had to about his feelings for Sadie. "I do."

"You took a bullet for her."

"I did, and I'd do it again."

"We researched you, you know," Sean informed him quietly.

"I didn't think you'd let Sadie stay with me if you hadn't." Chase didn't know where the other man was going with this conversation, but he wasn't prepared for his next words.

"I know about what happened with the Delta Force team you were imbedded with over in the Middle East."

Chase was stunned into silence. He knew? How in the hell did Sean find out about *that*?

"Jackson?" Ghost asked from next to him, obviously picking up on his nonverbal body language.

Chase waved his hand at Ghost, letting him know he was all right.

Sean Taggart went on. "I'm sorry that shit happened to you, but I have a feeling it made you a better soldier."

Chase didn't know what to say to that, so he said nothing as the other man continued.

"All I'm asking is that you treat Sadie right. Being married to a military man is never easy, but someone like you, who isn't exactly Special Forces but still works with the worst of the worst, and could still be targeted by terrorists, doesn't exactly have a life filled with sunshine and roses. But I know my niece. She's tough. And loyal. Very loyal. Look at what happened with Milena. Even when the shit hit the fan with the school, she didn't leave. She stayed to help and offer moral support. And instead of saving her own ass when things went to shit after they were snatched, she did what she could to help Milena. All I'm saying is that I'm glad she found a man like you."

Chase's chin fell to his chest in relief. It wasn't that he needed Sean's approval, but he sure was glad he had it. "Thanks. Means a lot."

"But if you hurt her, there's nowhere on this planet you can hide from me or my brothers," Sean concluded.

Chase couldn't help it. He chuckled. *That* was what he'd expected Sean to say when he claimed Sadie as his. "Right. Glad we got that out of the way."

"You need an extra set of eyes or ears?"

Chase wanted to say no, but when it came to protecting Sadie, he'd never turn down a former Special Forces soldier. "If you've got someone, it would help."

"Me and Ian'll be down tomorrow."

Chase blinked. He'd sorta expected Sean to send one of the younger members of the McKay-Taggart group. Or even one of the unattached men. But when he thought about it, he wasn't surprised. If it was Rayne who was in trouble, or one of her children, he wouldn't trust anyone else to keep her safe. "We'll be at Fletch's. We're having a small get-together tonight. We were going to barbeque outside, but now we'll keep everyone hunkered down inside."

"Jonathan won't try to burn the place down with all you in it, will he? You don't want to make it easier for him to take you all out."

Chase had thought about that too. "If you want my opinion, whatever happened inside that room has made him even more focused on Sadie. Yeah, he's not happy with me. Enough to fucking try to kill me instead of Sadie, but I really don't think anyone else is in danger. He's a coward at heart. Showing up and confronting more than just Sadie isn't his style. When the shit hit the fan at the school, he and his father ran. I'm fairly certain he'll wait and try to ambush me and steal Sadie when we least expect it. Just like he did at that nightclub when he got his hands on Milena and Sadie."

"I agree. But that doesn't mean you shouldn't be cautious," Sean warned.

"Which is why we're staying inside tonight, and why me and Sadie will stay at Fletch's house rather than in the apartment over his garage," Chase shot back. "When it comes to Jonathan, there's safety in numbers."

With what sounded like respect, Sean said, "Right. I'll see you first thing tomorrow then. Tell Sadie her aunt and I love her."

"Will do."

"Later."

"Bye."

Chase clicked off his phone, closed his eyes, and rested his head on the headrest.

"Sean Taggart is coming down?" Ghost asked.

"And his brother, Ian," Chase told him.

Ghost grinned. "I've always wanted to work with those guys."

Chase huffed out a laugh but didn't open his eyes. Leave it to Ghost to get excited about working with some of the most notorious badasses in the country. He wouldn't be surprised if the Taggarts tried to recruit members of the Delta Force team at some point in the future.

Opening his eyes when he felt the vehicle slow, Chase saw that they were pulling into Fletch's driveway. The Highlander Fletch drove the women home in was nowhere to be seen, but Chase wasn't worried. He knew he and Ghost would've been notified if something went wrong with the trip home.

Ghost pulled up next to the garage, turned off the engine, and got out. Chase followed suit.

They were walking toward the house when the front door flew open.

Sadie ran out of the house, and Chase frowned. He didn't like that she wasn't paying attention to her surroundings. He *did* like that he seemed to be the object of her attention at the moment, but he needed her to be more self-aware. Jonathan would wait for a moment just like this one to strike.

He opened his mouth to tell her to get back inside when she stopped in her tracks. They were about ten feet apart and she stood stock still, her mouth open, her face paling.

It wasn't until she swayed on her feet that Chase realized something was wrong. He rushed toward her and heard her say, "Your arm," before her eyes rolled back in her head and she passed out, falling to the ground in a heap before Chase could get to her.

Chapter Seven

Sadie shifted on the bed, not understanding why her mattress was so lumpy. She opened her eyes and winced at the bright light. She turned her head to the side—and froze.

Chase was sitting next to her, looking down at her in concern.

She wrinkled her brow. "What are you doing in my bedroom?"

If anything, her question made him look even more concerned. "We're at Fletch's house, Sparky. Not your bedroom."

It all came back to her in a rush then. She sat up, nearly whacking Chase in the head in the process. "Your arm! Are you okay? Oh my God, I had no idea he'd hit you!"

"I'm fine."

"You're not fine," Sadie insisted. "You're bleeding! Your shirt was soaked with it. Did you go to the hospital? How long have I been sleeping?"

"First of all, you weren't sleeping. You passed out. You fell right to the ground before I could get to you. Second, I didn't go to the hospital because there was no need. I knew Fletch would sew me up if I needed it. Third, you've been in here about an hour. I wouldn't let anyone disturb you."

Sadie's eyes went to his sleeve. He was wearing a different shirt than he'd had on earlier. This one was a short-sleeve gray Army PT shirt. She knew because the guys at McKay-Taggart wore them all the time. There was a white bandage over his left biceps. Without thought, her fingers moved to it. "Can I see?"

Chase put his hand over hers, halting her movements. "I'm fine," he repeated.

"Let me see." It wasn't a question that time.

Sighing, as if he knew she wouldn't stop asking until he gave in, Chase turned so she had better access to his wound and let her do what she wanted.

Sadie pulled the tape off of the gauze and peeled it down. There was a definite gouge in the flesh of his upper arm. The bullet had taken a chunk of skin, but it didn't look like it had done too much damage…even though it had bled a lot. Pressing the tape back into place, Sadie said, "I'm usually not so squeamish. I've seen my share of blood and gunshots, but it's just that…it was you. And you were shot because of *me*."

"Sparky," Chase warned.

"It was Jonathan," Sadie blurted before Chase could say anything else.

"I heard you warn me a second before he shot. I wasn't sure if you had actually seen him or not," Chase said.

"I saw him. He was crouched behind a car."

"You got a good look at him?" Chase asked.

"Oh yeah. He looked right at me," Sadie said. "I'm sorry, Chase. I'm so sorry!"

"Shut up," he told her in a gentle tone. "This isn't your fault. I'm just glad it was me and not you."

"Don't say that!" she exclaimed. "Don't fucking say that. How would you feel if our positions were reversed? Do you think it would make you feel better if I was shot instead of you?"

"Fuck no," he bit out.

"Right. So don't think that it makes *me* feel any better."

They stared at each other for a long moment before Chase reached for her. He pulled her into his arms and said, "I'm sorry. You're right. Nothing about this situation is cool."

They sat there together for a long moment before Chase drew back and informed her, "Sean and Ian are coming down tomorrow."

Sadie sighed. "I'd prefer they weren't involved."

"There's no way they're staying away."

"I know that too. But them coming down makes it more real for me."

"Makes what more real, Sparky?" Chase asked.

"The threat. I could tell myself that it wasn't that big of a deal when it was just you watching me. I could tell myself that Jonathan had left the state and all this craziness was for naught. But I know my uncles. If they're on their way, they're worried, and they'll keep me locked up until they find Jonathan."

"They love you."

"And I love them. But I hate this. *Hate*."

"Think of it this way," Chase said. "If Jonathan hadn't made a move, we might not've known he was here already. We might've gotten even more complacent and he might've had a chance to snatch you right out from under my nose. So Sean and Ian coming down here means that this will end sooner rather than later. I have no doubt they'll be a huge help in capturing that asshole."

"Yeah."

"They will."

"I know."

"Why don't you sound happy about that?" Chase asked.

Sadie bit her lip as she looked into Chase's brown eyes. He'd been hurt because of her. Because of what she'd done. Oh, she knew Jonathan had been the one to pull the trigger today, but he was there because of her actions. He was determined to punish her for tricking him when they were in that bedroom at Bexar.

If Jonathan got his hands on her again, she knew he'd kill her.

Her feelings for Chase were complicated, but no matter how many times they butted heads, she respected him...liked him. More than liked him. *Wanted* him.

Taking a deep breath and trying to be brave, she said, "Because once Jonathan is captured, I'll have to go back to Dallas. Back to my life."

Chase slowly moved his hand and speared his fingers into her hair until he was palming her head. He caressed her cheek with his thumb. "If you think I'm going to let you go home and not see you again, you're wrong."

Sadie blinked. She knew she was leaning into his hand but couldn't stop herself. "Really?"

"Really. You heard me when I told you that you're mine, didn't you?"

Her hopes rose and she nodded. "I thought maybe you were just caught up in the moment or something." Then she held her breath as

Chase leaned toward her. She kept her eyes on his, not willing to close them and miss a second of her first kiss with the man she was falling in love with.

She licked her lips in anticipation of his kiss…

But before their lips met, the door opened. "Is she awake yet— Oh…sorry," Rayne said, not sounding sorry at all. "We're downstairs waiting on you guys. Annie's about to burst with curiosity. She wants to examine your wound, Chase. Just a friendly warning. And Sadie, us ladies want to know more about the hot guys who work for McKay-Taggart."

"Jeez, sis, you're practically married," Chase said with a groan.

"But I'm not dead. I'm allowed to look at good-looking men! Now come on. Quit sucking face and come downstairs and join the rest of us." And with that, Rayne shut the door.

Sadie bit her lip and looked up at Chase. "Guess we better go before she sics Annie on us."

Chase ran his thumb over her glistening lips as he said, "We're staying over here tonight. Fletch and Emily already went over to the apartment and got our stuff. We'll eat, then we'll talk about Jonathan and the school. Then we'll finish what we didn't get to start a second ago."

Sadie knew she was blushing but nodded anyway. She didn't want to tell him about Jonathan, but she needed to before she got in over her head. Which was a joke, because she *already* felt in over her head with Chase. But she needed to see his reaction to what she'd done, and he needed to know why Jonathan was so determined to get to her. If Chase still wanted to be with her after he knew everything, it would be that much better.

"That work for you?" Chase asked. She'd obviously taken too long to answer.

"Yeah, Chase. That works for me."

"I'll say it now and I'll say it again later if you need to hear it. In fact, I'll keep saying it until you believe me. Whatever happened doesn't make a damn bit of difference to me. It kept you alive and it kept you safe. So you don't need to be concerned about how I'm going to react when you tell me whatever horrible thing you think you've done. I can guarantee you it's not going to change the way I feel about you. It's not going to make me want you less."

Sadie stared at him.

"That's right, Sparky. I want you. I've wanted you from the moment I saw you. I shouldn't have waited in the first place, but I figured we'd have time. Which was stupid. I know better than anyone how fleeting life can be. I watched an entire squad of good men, some of the best I've known, die in an instant. I don't ever want to have any regrets, and having something happen to you before I can make you mine would definitely make me regret not speaking up. I'm just hoping you'll give me a chance to show you that I can be the man for you."

Sadie swallowed and opened her mouth to spill her guts. To tell him she'd wanted him the first time she saw him as well. That she would give up all her worldly possessions if *he* gave *her* the chance to show him that she could be the woman for him.

But the door to the room opened before she could say anything and little Annie entered.

"Come *on*," she whined. "We can't start eating without you guys and I'm starrrrrving! I'm gonna *die* if I don't get a hotdog in the next thirty seconds!"

Chase kept his hand on Sadie's face for a beat before leaning forward and kissing her forehead gently. Then he stood and held out his hand, his good one, for Sadie. She slid off the mattress and timidly placed her hand in his. After what he'd said, she felt shy for some reason.

"All right, Annie. We're comin'. Lead the way," Chase told the little girl.

She marched toward them and got behind him. Then she put both hands on his butt and pushed. "Daddy told me not to leave the room without you. So *you* have to lead the way."

Chase chuckled. "Smart man," he murmured under his breath, but allowed himself to be pushed out of the bedroom.

Sadie followed along in his wake, smiling at the antics of Fletch's little girl. She was precocious and adorable at the same time.

Chapter Eight

Dinner went surprisingly well. Sadie had thought she might be uncomfortable with Ghost and Fletch, but they were down to earth and reminded her a lot of the operatives who worked for McKay-Taggart. She had friends, but sitting around watching Rayne and Emily interact with each other and their men was refreshing. They showed their love for one another openly. They teased and laughed together, but it was absolutely done out of affection and respect.

Too many times in college Sadie had lost friends because of petty jealousies and perceived competition on their part. But it was obvious Emily and Rayne weren't envious of each other. Maybe it was because they were older, maybe it was because they were with soldiers who they knew could be killed on any of their missions. Whatever it was, Sadie liked them. She enjoyed being a part of their inner circle. She wanted to have that true intimacy with another woman, or a group of women. She felt as if she had it with Milena and had missed relaxing and chatting with her over the last month. It was always great to have a boyfriend, but there was just something different about knowing you had women you could count on no matter what.

They were sitting around relaxing and talking after dinner when Ghost's phone rang. He obviously recognized the number and didn't care if the others overheard his conversation, because he didn't bother getting off the couch to answer it.

"Ghost here. Hey, Fish, how are you? How's Bryn?" He smiled at the group as he listened to whatever was being said on the other end of the line.

"Really? She said that? Shit, I love your wife, man. She's awesome."

Sadie felt Chase stiffen next to her right after Ghost began speaking, but she didn't know why. Chase had the hand of his injured arm sitting on her thigh, as if they sat like that all the time, but for whatever reason, when Ghost started talking to his friend, his fingers dug into her leg almost painfully.

She looked over at him—and he was staring at Ghost with a gaze that was as intense as she'd ever seen. "Chase?" she asked softly, getting concerned.

Ghost was still talking. "When you get that new prosthetic, let us know. I'm interested to hear how you like it and if it's as high tech as it's purported to be. Annie says she misses you. She's upset we got to come out and see you not too long ago. After she heard all about Bryn, she can't wait to meet her."

"What's his last name?" Chase asked loudly, making Sadie jump. He wasn't trying to be polite; he'd barged into Ghost's conversation as if he had every right. He sounded pissed too. As if he was angry that Ghost was on the phone in the first place.

Sadie looked at Chase. His teeth were obviously grinding because she could see his jaw flexing. His lips were pressed together and his eyes were narrowed. He was still gripping her leg hard enough that she'd probably have bruises. Sadie wanted to do something to help him, but she wasn't sure what was wrong in the first place.

Ghost went from relaxed and jovial to irritated—and possibly a little angry—in a heartbeat. "Hang on," he said into the phone, then held it against his chest and stared at Chase. "What's *your* problem?"

"You called whoever you're talking to 'Fish.' What's his last name?"

Ghost didn't answer immediately, and the two men stared at each other for a long moment.

Rayne finally broke the tense silence. "Munroe. Fish's name is Dane Munroe. Why? What's going on, Chase?"

Sadie watched as all the blood drained from Chase's face, as if he'd just seen a ghost. She didn't understand what in the world was going on, but it was something big.

As if in a trance, Chase held out his hand to Ghost, obviously asking for the phone.

"Chase?" Rayne asked again, sounding extremely concerned now.

Ghost hesitated for a second, but whatever he saw in Chase's face made him lean forward and hand him the phone.

Everyone in the room was silent, aware that something big was happening, but not sure what.

Sadie reached over and put her hand on Chase's leg, but she didn't think he even knew she was there. Hell, she didn't think he was aware of anyone around him.

He slowly brought the phone up to his ear. Sadie could hear the man named Fish on the other end; his voice was loud and easily heard through the speaker of the phone since she was sitting right next to Chase.

"Hello?" Chase said tentatively.

"Who's this?" Fish asked.

"Captain Chase Jackson. Who's this?"

There was a long pause on the other end of the line, then Fish asked, "No shit? *Jackson?*"

"Yeah. Please tell me you are who I think you are."

"Fuck me. Goddamn. I can't fucking believe this!"

Sadie's eyes widened at the amount of swear words coming from whoever Chase was talking to. He sounded almost as shaken up as Chase looked.

Finally, when he'd apparently run out of dirty words, he simply said, "I thought you were dead, man."

Chase huffed out a breath and closed his eyes. "I thought *you* were dead. Is there anyone else?"

Fish cleared his throat. "No. I'm the only one. Ghost and his team came across the convoy and saved my life. Lost my arm, but if Truck hadn't clamped my artery for the forty minutes it took to get to a medic station, I would've lost my life too. Shit, Sir…if I had known…I… They would've gotten you out too. I thought you were *dead.*"

The emotion on Chase's face was clear for everyone in the room to see. No one said a word; even little Annie was quiet as they all watched whatever was happening play out in front of them.

"They did the right thing. I passed out and when I woke up, you were gone. Thought the locals had gotten ahold of you," Chase told Fish. "Jesus, Munroe. I just can't… I can't believe you're alive."

A tear fell down Sadie's cheek, but she didn't wipe it away. The mixture of joy and sorrow on Chase's face was both beautiful and heartbreaking at the same time. She knew Fish must be one of the soldiers from the group who were going to rescue the hostage. She remembered Chase's anguish when he'd talked about how all the men had died in the explosion, and how he hadn't been able to find any information on them.

"Where are you?" Chase asked.

"Idaho."

"Idaho? What the hell are you doing all the way out there?"

"Long story, but basically, I needed to get away from everything. Can't be around large groups of people anymore. Loud sounds bother me. It suits me out here. Best decision I ever made. I met my wife after I moved."

Chase's eyes closed and his head bowed. He struggled with emotion before opening his eyes and staring over at Ghost and Fletch. "Fucking pleased, Munroe. You have no idea."

Belatedly, Fletch put his hands over Annie's ears as if he could block out the word she just heard.

"Yeah, Sir, I do," was Fish's response.

"I'd like to come visit sometime…if that's all right," Chase said hesitantly.

"Yes. Absolutely, yes. You can meet Bryn, my wife. She's hysterical and super smart. I mean, *really* smart. But don't get any ideas… I know you work in counterterrorism. I won't let her get into that shit. You'll understand why when you meet her. She gets *too* into it and doesn't know when to let stuff go."

"I can't wait to meet her. I'm gonna give you back to Ghost now."

"Okay. Sir?"

"Yeah?"

"I'm glad you're not dead," Fish told him.

"Right back at'cha," Chase replied. Then he held the phone out to Ghost. The other man took it, and he and Fish had a short conversation before he hung up.

"You were there that day?" Ghost asked in a low tone.

Chase nodded. "I'd been assigned to the team on a special mission. It was all hush-hush. A part of counterterrorism intel gathering. We were supposed to go in and rescue that female truck driver who'd been taken hostage."

Fletch spoke next. "Jeez, man… We checked everyone. How did we miss you?"

Chase shrugged. "When I came to the first time, I realized that the truck seat had landed on top of me. I had to literally dig my way out later. I think with my brown hair and the way I was covered in dirt…I just blended into the landscape. I'm not surprised you missed me."

Ghost shook his head. "I can't believe I left my future brother-in-law there to die. No. Not acceptable. We fucked up. You could've been captured by the same people who took the truck driver."

"But I wasn't. Quit beating yourself up." Chase's gaze met first Fletch's then Ghost's. "That's an order," he said. Then his voice lowered. "Munroe is alive. It's a miracle. I thought I was the only one."

Rayne asked, "How in the world did you not know about Fish? I mean, he was around when that shit happened with Kassie. He was even at Emily's wedding. I know you didn't go, but still. He was here. And haven't I talked about him around you? It's not like you're living in a bubble."

Chase looked over at his sister. "I don't know. We talk, but I haven't told anyone about that mission…well, except for Sadie, and that was really recently. I don't hang out with Ghost and the others too often because of fraternization rules. The Army doesn't think much of enlisted soldiers hanging with officers."

"Well, that's just stupid," Rayne said under her breath.

Chase smiled but went on. "Thank you," he said, looking at both of the Delta Force operatives. "Thank you for finding Munroe and getting him out of there. Thank you for what you do, and especially thank you for helping me keep Sadie safe."

"Fuck that," Ghost said. "You don't have to thank us. This is what we do."

"Exactly," Fletch agreed.

"And Fish would've done the same exact thing if the roles had been reversed," Ghost said.

"Damn straight," Fletch agreed.

"And I know he's not here, but please thank Truck for me," Chase said, looking at Ghost, "for not giving up on Munroe. I don't know all the details, only what he told me on the phone just now, but you guys could've easily given up. Figured he'd bleed to death, but you didn't. Knowing one of those men is alive today…and happily married…I just… I don't have the words."

"Sir," Ghost began, leaning forward, resting his elbows on his knees. His intense gaze met Chase's. "Truck would totally say this if he was here too. You *don't* have to thank us. So don't do it again. If any of those other men had even a one-in-one-hundred shot at making it out of there alive, we would've taken it. The fact that Fish was bleeding out and would obviously lose his arm only made us all the more determined to save his life. And if we'd have found you there, we would've done the same thing for you."

The atmosphere in the room was charged. Everyone's emotions were running high.

As if she knew the mood needed to be lightened, Annie climbed off of Fletch's lap and walked over to Chase. She didn't ask, simply climbed onto *his* lap and put her hands on both his cheeks.

Sadie smiled and moved over, giving the little girl some room.

Annie leaned in and rubbed her nose against Chase's, then sat back, leaving her hands on his face, and said, "Next time, don't sleep through my daddy coming to rescue you."

Everyone burst out laughing.

Somehow Chase managed to keep it together, and he brought his hands up to Annie's head and pulled her toward him so he could kiss her on the forehead. "I won't. Thanks, Annie."

And with that, Annie nodded and scooted off his knees. She padded back over to Fletch and he lifted her back up to his lap.

Sadie pushed an arm behind Chase and rested her hand on his hip, then curled her legs up onto the couch. She leaned into him and put her free hand on his chest. He covered it with one of his own and carefully wrapped his injured arm around her back.

He inhaled, then let out a huge sigh, and Sadie felt him melt against her, as if all the worries he'd been holding in had been released with his breath. The knowledge that one of the men he'd thought dead was not only alive, but happily married, was obviously enough to help him let go of some of the tension he'd been holding on to.

Talk turned to general, everyday matters, until it finally came back around to Jonathan, and the reason she and Chase were in the house in the first place.

"We need to talk about Jonathan," Chase said, but looked pointedly at Fletch and Annie with his eyebrows raised.

Getting the hint, Emily stood up and said, "And with that, I think it's time for Annie to get to bed."

"But, Mom," the little girl complained, "I wanna hear the stramagy for keeping the bad guy away from Sadie!"

"When you're a soldier in your own right, you can be in on strategy meetings," Fletch told her. "But for now, it's past your bedtime and you need to get some sleep."

She whined a bit more, obviously tired, but eventually allowed her mom to help her off Fletch's lap and lead her to her room.

"Should I go too?" Rayne asked quietly from beside Ghost.

Chase shook his head. "No, I think you need to hear this. The last thing we want is to leave you, Emily, and Annie vulnerable to this asshole."

Sadie shivered and felt Chase's arm tighten around her.

"Here's the deal. Sadie's uncle is coming down tomorrow with Ian Taggart. Simply having those two around will go a long way toward giving us the upper hand. They were Special Forces as well, and they're badass. And Sadie is certain that was Jonathan today. He flattened all four of my tires and disabled my car in the parking lot to give him a chance to get to her."

"How'd he find out she was here?" Ghost asked.

"I'm not sure. I'm guessing that maybe there are still some officers down in San Antonio who used to visit the school that weren't caught in the aftermath of the bust. It's possible he could be blackmailing them to get information on Sadie's whereabouts."

"Why does he want you so badly?" Rayne asked.

Sadie bit her lip and looked down at her lap. She didn't want to tell *Chase*; there was no way she was telling her new friend and the Deltas.

Luckily, Chase came to her rescue. "It doesn't matter. It only matters that he does. So let's talk scenarios."

Sadie squeezed Chase's waist in silent thanks and he gripped her hand at his chest in reply. She relaxed further into his side, feeling connected to him in a way she hadn't felt with anyone in a really long time.

Emily returned after getting Annie settled and immediately went to her husband. She took Annie's spot on his lap and the conversation continued.

The discussion was fast and furious, ideas and thoughts mostly coming from the men. They discussed ways to keep Sadie, and the other women, safe from Jonathan, what they thought he might do if, God forbid, he got his hands on any of them. They talked about what the women should do if they found themselves taken hostage by the man. Finally, they made a plan on what they should do if Jonathan wasn't captured in the next couple of days. The last thing anyone wanted was for the threat from the man to drag on for weeks or months.

Sadie knew offering herself up as bait would be the perfect solution to the situation, but she also knew Chase, not to mention her uncles, wouldn't let her.

As if he could read her mind, Fletch said, "This is just a suggestion—I wouldn't be doing my job if I didn't at least throw it out there—what if we had Sadie go somewhere by herself? We could watch her from a distance and if Jonathan showed up, we could grab him."

Interestingly, it wasn't Chase who replied first, but Ghost. "No fucking way."

"We'd be there watching her; so would the Taggarts. Nothing would happen to her."

"We don't put one of our own in harm's way. Period. Besides, Jonathan might be a pedophile and batshit crazy, but that doesn't mean he's stupid. He would know it's a trap. She was with Chase today, and not too long after he tried to take him out, Fletch and I showed up. He knows she has a protection detail. Besides, would you want Emily in that situation? Maybe we should send Annie to the park by herself?"

"No, that's not—" Fletch began, but was interrupted by Ghost.

"Right. Just because Sadie is new to our group doesn't mean she's expendable. She fucking is not."

Sadie's eyes filled with tears upon hearing Ghost defending her. It was true, he didn't know her, nor did any of the other men and women in the room, but it didn't matter. He wasn't going to let her put herself in danger just to end the threat to the others.

She started, realizing for the first time that if she were to be Chase's—*really* be Chase's—then Ghost could end up being her brother-in-law and Rayne would be her sister-in-law.

She suddenly wanted that. With every fiber of her being. But she was definitely jumping the gun. She hadn't even kissed Chase. It was silly to be thinking about marriage…wasn't it?

Maybe not, considering how many times Chase had said she was his and that he wanted her. He'd even flat-out said he wanted to marry her.

Looking up at Chase, Sadie blinked at the emotion she saw on his face. He was staring at Fletch with his eyes narrowed and his lips pursed.

He was apparently upset with him for even suggesting that they use her as bait. She'd thought he was intense when he was talking to that Fish guy on the phone. But that was nothing compared to what she was seeing right this moment.

"You're right," Fletch said, then turned to Sadie. "And I apologize to you too. I wasn't really saying we should use you like that, I was just brainstorming. Trying to think of ways we could get you safe as fast as possible."

She nodded at the man. She didn't think badly of him; she was actually surprised no one had brought it up earlier.

After another hour, the men seemed to agree on a plan of sorts. It all hinged on Jonathan and how crazy he was. Sadie had a feeling that Jonathan would make a move sooner rather than later. He was pissed. And obsessed. Those things alone would make him desperate to get his hands on her, and hopefully he'd walk right into the trap the Deltas were laying.

"Emily's out," Fletch said softly. "She has a tendency to conk out because of the pregnancy. I'm going to take her to bed." His wife had moved to lie on the couch next to him and was dead to the world. Even though she was tall, she looked almost petite sleeping next to her muscular husband.

"I'm half asleep too," Rayne told Ghost, yawing as if to emphasize her point.

As the group began to break up, Fletch came over to where Sadie was sitting with Chase. He squatted down in front of her and said, "I'm sorry if I hurt your feelings, Sadie. I didn't think it was the best idea, but I was just trying to think of something that would help end this for you."

She hadn't been expecting him to apologize again, so she didn't say anything. Chase answered before she could think of a reply.

"Don't do that shit again, Fletch. I get that in the past, offering people up as bait was something your team discussed, and even did, but those times are gone. Too many of us have our own women to even consider that a viable option anymore."

"You're right. It was a dick thing to even suggest, given the circumstances."

When neither man said anything else, Sadie knew she had to end the pseudo standoff. She put her hand on Fletch's arm. "It's okay. I understand, I do." She gave him a small nod.

"We'll keep you safe, Sadie. We're trained in this shit. You worked at McKay-Taggart for a while before you went to San Antonio, right? I'm guessing the operatives up there were just as protective of their spouses as we are with ours," Fletch said.

Sadie nodded. She *did* know. Ian and the others always looked after their significant others. And if she was being honest with herself, it was pretty awesome knowing she had someone to lean on, to help her make decisions about important things in her life, and who would stand up for her and protect her if push came to shove. "I understand," she told Fletch.

He nodded and stood, then held out a hand to help her stand, and Sadie took it. Chase was by her side immediately, taking her hand from Fletch's. She would've laughed but didn't have it in her.

"We'll see you in the morning," Chase said. "You're taking first watch?"

"Yeah. I'll get Emily settled, and I'll wake Ghost up in an hour."

"Sounds good."

"Later, Sir."

As they were walking to their room, Sadie asked Chase, "Why do they call you 'Sir'?"

"To make a long story short, other than Ghost, they're enlisted and I'm an officer. It's engrained in all of us to talk to each other that way. Even though I'm friends with them, it's technically illegal for me to hang out and be buddy-buddy with them."

"That *is* stupid," Sadie said. "I don't get it."

"Think about it this way," Chase tried to explain. "If we have to go into combat together, I'll be giving the orders. They're expected to carry out those orders without question. If we're friends, I might either not give the appropriate order to go into battle because I don't want to see my friends hurt, or they might question my authority because of our personal relationship. It's a sticky situation, and the reason the no-fraternization rule is in effect."

Chase closed the bedroom door behind him as he finished speaking.

"Yeah, okay. That makes sense. But it sucks. Because I want you guys to all be friends. They're all awesome people."

"Yup. But when Ghost marries my sister, we'll be legally related, so that means the Army probably won't let us work together in any capacity. And since he has no intention of leaving his team, that means I won't have to worry about commanding Fletch, Truck, and the others. So I have no heartburn about staying here tonight, or any other night, or with working with them to keep you safe."

"That's good."

"Yeah, Sparky, that's good. Now, why don't you get ready for bed? We'll talk, then we'll see if we can't pick up where we left off when Annie interrupted earlier."

"You still want to?" she asked.

Chase leaned in, and Sadie inhaled his unique peppermint scent. He brought his hand up to the side of her neck and she shivered as his light touch made goose bumps break out on her arms. "I still want to. Even though we were discussing ways to keep you safe downstairs, the only thing I could think about was bringing you back up here, laying you on this bed, and showing you exactly how much you mean to me."

Sadie could only stare at him. She'd dreamed about hearing something like that from him almost since she'd met him. Now, she could hardly believe he'd actually said it.

"Go get changed. I left you something to wear to bed in the bathroom. I'll go use the guest bathroom down the hall."

Then, without warning, he moved in close and covered her lips with his own.

Surprised, Sadie gasped, and he took advantage of her shock, pressing his tongue into her mouth. His kiss wasn't tentative. Wasn't a first-kiss, let-me-see-what-she-might-like exploration. He devoured her. Holding the back of her head with his hand and not letting her pull away, not that she wanted to.

After the initial shock, Sadie moaned and gave him what he wanted. She opened wider and tilted her head, allowing him to consume her.

He pulled back after several moments of intense kissing and stared at her. He licked his lips and took a deep breath. "Go get ready for bed, Sparky."

"Okay," she whispered, but neither of them moved.

He finally huffed out a short laugh and stepped away from her. "Go on. If you don't go now, I won't be able to get control of myself and we won't talk first."

"Maybe we can skip the talk," Sadie said hopefully. Making love with Chase sounded much better than talking about Jonathan.

"Talk first, then I'm going to make love with you for the rest of the night. I want to know where you're the most sensitive, how and where you like to be touched, and what you taste like."

"Chase," Sadie breathed, her knees weak from the imagery his words evoked.

Without another word, Chase spun and left the room.

Sadie brought a hand up to her lips and traced them. Then she smiled and hurried to the bathroom to get ready for bed.

He might not have meant it as such, but that kiss was as good an incentive to talk as she'd ever had. She'd tell Chase about Jonathan, hopefully he would still want to be with her, then she'd finally have the man she'd been lusting after for way too long.

The day had kinda sucked, but if it ended with Chase inside her, she'd relive it in a heartbeat.

Chapter Nine

Chase lay on the bed waiting for Sadie to come out of the bathroom. She'd been in there a while, but he wasn't going to rush her. It was bad enough he'd kissed her like he had, not to mention telling her he wanted to make love to her all night.

He hadn't lied, though he probably shouldn't have been so blunt. But sitting next to her all night, breathing in her scent and holding her in his arms, had gotten him so worked up, he couldn't have held back if his life depended on it.

She probably thought he'd tuned her out completely when he was talking to Munroe. That he had no idea she'd been stroking his leg with comforting motions while he'd barely held himself together. Finding out that he *hadn't* been the only man to survive that fucked-up mission had been surprising, exhilarating, and frustrating all at the same time. His commanding officer should've told him. He understood that the deaths of an entire Delta Force team was kept on a need-to-know-basis…but fuck that. *He'd* needed to know. He'd thought for months that every one of those Delta Force soldiers had died at the hands of ISIS. The guilt he'd felt for being the only one to walk away from that failed rescue mission had eaten at him.

He still mourned the other men who had died, but finding out Munroe was alive and well was a miracle.

Sadie had sat by him, not flinching away as he'd squeezed her leg, silently supporting him while he'd freaked out. It meant the world to him.

And he wanted that for the rest of his life. Her support. He'd take it and give it back tenfold. And only Sadie could give that kind of support to him. No one else would do. No one else could soothe him when he felt like he was drowning in an ocean of emotion. No one else could make him smile when he thought he'd never smile again.

He was done waiting.

He honestly didn't care anymore why Jonathan was obsessed with her. It didn't fucking matter what Sadie had or hadn't done. That asshole wasn't getting his hands on his woman. The past was the past, and whatever had happened when he'd had her in that bedroom at Bexar could die with Jonathan, for all Chase cared.

But it mattered to Sadie. He could see it in her eyes every time he looked at her. She was scared shitless that whatever she told him was going to send him running. But she had no clue. He wasn't going anywhere. He was hers, hopefully she was his, and that was that.

But in order for her to let it go, she had to get it off her chest. Had to tell him what happened so he could reassure her that he still wanted her…loved her…and they could move on. Once she told him, he'd show her in one of the most intimate ways he could that Jonathan fucking Jones would never come between them. Not then, not now, and never in the future.

Chase heard a noise and turned his head toward the bathroom. He inhaled sharply and felt his dick lengthen with arousal.

Sadie stood in the doorway of the bathroom, looking unsure. She was wearing his T-shirt, and it looked amazing on her. It was too big, of course, but since he wasn't that much taller than her, it hit her at the top of her thighs. He knew if she turned and bent over, he'd be able to see everything. He had no idea if she was wearing panties or not, but it didn't matter.

He held out a hand. "Come here, Sadie."

She tugged at the bottom of his T-shirt and shuffled over to the bed, biting her lip. The freckles on her face were almost obscured by the blush that shone brightly on her cheeks. He folded back the covers and smiled as Sadie hurriedly came forward and sat on the bed.

She lay back and he drew the covers up and over them both. The only light in the room was coming from a lamp on the other side of the bed. It cast a soft glow, enough so that he could see her face and gauge what she was thinking, but not so bright that it killed the mellow mood.

Chase pulled Sadie into him until she lay against his side with her head on his shoulder. This was the first time they'd lain together in a bed. Oh, he'd dreamed about it over the last month, but had controlled himself. It had almost killed him to say good night every evening and not follow her into his guest bedroom, but he'd done it. And now that he held her against him in bed? He wasn't ever going to let her sleep alone again.

He could feel her naked legs against his own and he ground his teeth to try to keep his erection under control. All he wanted to do was roll over on top of Sadie and make love to her until neither of them knew their names. He tried to tell himself to have patience.

"You okay?" he asked quietly.

She nodded against his shoulder.

Chase waited for a while, but when she didn't say anything more, he said, "Tell me about it." He didn't elaborate on what "it" was, figuring she knew.

He honestly thought Sadie had either fallen asleep or was going to ignore him, but finally she began to speak in a small, tired tone. "When I had my suspicions about what was going on at that school, I didn't hesitate to call my uncle. I figured he could probably do something. I was stupid for not telling Milena. I should've stopped her from going there day after day. But I knew how much the job meant to her, and she really cared about the teenagers she was looking after."

"You weren't one hundred percent sure what was going on, and being cautious wasn't a bad thing, Sparky."

She didn't comment but continued her story. "I went down there simply to visit and talked her into letting me come with her when she went to the school to work. She had no idea what was going on there, Chase. None."

Sadie's finger was making random patterns on his chest and Chase reached out and enfolded her hand in his own, trying to soothe her and encourage her at the same time.

"I didn't get a chance to see any of the younger girls when I was there. We weren't allowed to leave the area where the pregnant teens were housed. But after the raid, when the FBI agents were questioning me, I made them tell me what they could.

"Jeremiah and Jonathan were awful people. All the things they did to those poor girls were horrifying. And the fact that they basically rented them out for other pedophiles in the community just made it worse. I was so sickened by it all. Even though I was there for Milena, I felt as if I should've done something more to help those girls. The agents told me that Jeremiah had handpicked a group of girls for Jonathan. Told some they weren't lucky enough to be chosen by the leader, but being given to his son was almost as good. Others were castoffs of Jeremiah's who'd gotten too old for him."

Chase hated what he was hearing, but he honestly wasn't surprised. He'd sat in on the debriefing with the FBI about Jeremiah Jones and what the founder had been doing at the school. He'd read the transcripts of the interviews with some of the teenagers and girls who had been rescued. They were all going to need extensive therapy to overcome the brainwashing they'd been through.

He turned his head and put his lips on Sadie's forehead. Chase lay like that, letting his care and concern hopefully soak into her from their flesh-on-flesh contact. After a while, she continued.

"Even though I knew Jonathan was just as bad as his father, I wasn't really scared of him. I thought Milena was the one in danger, not me. When he kidnapped us, I honestly wasn't too worried. I mean, I was, but not for me. So when Jonathan dragged me away, it shocked me. I wasn't exactly thinking straight. It was so unreal when he started telling me what he wanted to do with me. That he wanted me as a breeder to give him baby girls he could molest to his heart's content.

"That nearly broke me. I could handle almost anything he did to me, but the thought of him taking my child and hurting her... It made me crazy. So, after he dragged me into a bedroom, and before he knocked me out, I...I let him touch me. He lifted my shirt and grabbed my boobs. He told me how ugly I was, and how fucking me would hurt both me *and* him. But the end result would be worth it."

Sadie looked up at him then, the pain, embarrassment, and shame shining bright in her eyes. "He hurt me, Chase. Twisted my nipples, squeezed my boobs, even put his hand on my throat to hold me down when I started to resist what he was doing. Said that he liked how easily he could mark my pale skin. That maybe he could learn to like fucking an older woman. He said he could hurt me more than he could the girls. That I could take more than they could. I...I didn't want to do it...but I knew I needed to stall him. Knew Milena's boyfriend would eventually come for her...so I had to do whatever I could to make sure he was distracted."

When she didn't continue, Chase pulled her on top of him, not wanting to trap her underneath him if she'd been raped by the bastard, and asked, "What, Sparky? What'd you do? Say it once, then we don't have to ever talk about it again."

Sadie closed her eyes and her breathing sped up. Chase recognized her reaction as a fight-or-flight response. He smoothed his hands over her skin lightly, not pressuring her to continue and not holding her against her will.

Finally, she said, "I pretended to orgasm while he was hurting me. I threw my head back and gave the performance of my life. Except the tears coming from my eyes weren't from ecstasy, but pain. And he bought it, hook, line, and sinker. I thought he was going to rip my pants off after I finished moaning and shaking like a porn star, but his touch gentled instead. He petted me for several minutes while I pretended to come down from my orgasmic high. Then he turned my head and made me kiss him. For a long time. I was still crying and shaking from the pain in my chest—but I made out with him. Kissed him as if I couldn't get enough, all the while trying not to gag. Then he reached for my hand and cuffed it to the bed. He sneered at me and said he knew I was a whore all along, just like all women were, and that he was going to enjoy hurting me in the future, but he was going to plant his seed inside me right then and there."

Sadie took a deep breath, then said, "But before he could do anything, his phone beeped with a text. I don't know who it was, maybe Jeremiah, but he knocked me out at that point. When I came to again, he dragged me out of that room down to another, where I saw Milena and her son. Jeremiah was holding JT, and he and Jonathan said goodbye to each other. Then Jonathan brought me back to the bedroom. He kissed me again, and I thought if I kissed him back, if I was docile, maybe I'd find a chance to get away. But he smiled at me. An evil, awful smile that made me want to puke. He told me he wanted to finish what he'd started earlier. He cuffed one of my wrists again then leaned over to grab something from a drawer in the table next to the bed.

"The thought of what he might have done to others on that same bed…of what he wanted to do to me…made me so *angry*! My foot was moving before I'd even thought about it. I kicked him with all my strength and he smashed his head on the table and fell over like a dead tree in the forest."

She closed her eyes then finished quickly. "I ripped off the Velcro cuff on my wrist. I didn't wait around to see if Jonathan was coming for me or not, I just ran out of there."

"You amaze me," Chase told her softly.

She shook her head. "I *kissed* him, Chase. I willingly let him touch me."

"Bullshit," he refuted. "You said it yourself, you were giving help time to get there. Giving *me* time to get to you. You were selfless and brave. You did what you had to do."

"You wouldn't be saying that if I'd slept with him. If he got me pregnant."

"Wrong," Chase said in a harsh voice. "Even if you didn't fight him, it still would've been rape. *He* was in the wrong, Sadie, not you. But you should know, even if he did take you, with or without your consent, even if you were pregnant as a result, it wouldn't change how I feel. Not one fucking bit. You're mine, Sadie Jennings. And any child you might've had as a result of that night would've been mine. *Ours.* Sparky, I don't care if you've slept with one man or a hundred. From this point on, you're mine. No one else exists for me."

"You can't really think that," Sadie argued. "All guys care how many men a woman has been with. Especially when one of those men could've been Jonathan."

"Would you think less of me if I told you I'd been with a hundred women? That I've had girlfriends since I was fifteen?"

"Well...no."

"Why not?"

"You're a guy. It's different."

"No. It's not different at all. It's fucking society that's convinced women it's okay if a man sleeps around and doesn't care about his virtue. It makes him a stud. But a woman has to guard her virginity like it's the eighteenth century, otherwise she's a slut and a whore."

Sadie stared at him with wide eyes. He saw the moment his point sank home.

"I see you're getting it. Look, we all have pasts. Good, bad, and ugly. There are things I wish I'd done differently growing up, but I can't change any of it. All I can do is go forward. But you making a conscious decision to do what you needed to in order to buy yourself and Milena some time isn't something you should *ever* be ashamed of."

She dropped her head and it thumped down onto his shoulder. She scrunched her arms under her and laid her palms flat on his chest. Her legs separated and she straddled his hips, drawing her knees up next to his body. Chase folded his arms around her.

Several minutes passed and neither said a word. They just enjoyed being close to one another.

Finally, Sadie lifted her head. "He hurt me, and I was afraid it would be a really long time before I wanted to be with someone else. Or even wanted to be around men in general. But from the second I saw you, I knew you were different."

"I *am* different," Chase said immediately.

She grinned, and he was so relieved he would've given her the moon if only she'd keep smiling at him like that. "You're mine."

"Yeah, Sparky, I am. And I hope you already know this, but I won't ever hurt you like that asshole did. Not ever."

"I know. I wouldn't be here if I thought different."

"So is that why you think Jonathan wants you so badly?" Chase asked, wanting to get the subject completely done with before they moved on. "Because you bested him?"

Sadie shrugged. "Maybe. I think he thinks I betrayed him in some way. Pretending to orgasm and kissing him made him think I wanted him. But when I kicked him, he must have realized it was all a lie. He's obsessed with me. Or the babies he thinks I can give him. I think he's built up this fantasy in his mind about starting a new school and having red-haired little girls following him, at his beck and call for his perverted urges. And he's convinced I'm the only one who can give them to him."

"Yeah, I think you're right. He probably feels like you're his possession. He grew up under his father's thumb, so he sees women as being good for one thing and one thing only. Instead of disappearing, which he should have done, since the FBI is looking for him, he can't get past losing you."

Sadie shivered over him, and Chase would've smacked himself on the back of his own head if he could've. "I'm sorry, Sparky. I don't need to continue talking about this."

She immediately shook her head. "No. You aren't saying anything I haven't thought about myself. But I think it's more than that. I tricked him. Pretended to like what he did. I think I hurt his ego, because I made him look stupid and because I got away from him."

Chase nodded. "Yeah, I can see how that might make him even more obsessive."

"I just…I really want him to leave me alone."

"It's better this way," Chase said, then hurried to explain when she stiffened. "Think about it. What if he did disappear? If he'd gone to Mexico to hide out? He'd still be feeling the same way he does now. Possessive and like he owns you. But we wouldn't know about it. You'd go about your life and not worry about him, thinking he was long gone. But then one day he could just waltz back into town and grab you."

"You're right," Sadie agreed immediately, then shuddered. "When you put it that way, I'm totally glad he's impatient, immature, and slightly insane."

Chase carefully turned, keeping Sadie tucked into him until she was on her back and he was over her, resting his weight on his elbows. He tangled his fingers in her hair and held her head still. "You good?"

"Good?"

"Not worried over what I'm going to think about what you had to do in that room with that asshole?"

She dropped her eyes, then bit her lip as she looked back up at him. "You really don't think less of me for letting him touch me?"

"No, Sparky. Not even a smidge. In fact, hearing about what happened from your perspective only makes me think more highly of you."

For several seconds neither of them said a word, then Sadie whispered, "Make love to me?"

"If I do anything that makes you uncomfortable, you tell me," Chase ordered. "If I touch you and it brings back too many bad memories, say something. If we start this and you panic, tell me. I don't care if I'm inside you and you have a flashback, you say the word and I'll stop. The last thing I want is this to be something you're tolerating rather than something you want more than your next breath…which is how I want you."

"Chase…" Sadie said, her voice breaking.

"You promise?" Chase pushed.

"I promise. I want you. Have from the moment I saw you. Please, make love to me."

"Nothing would please me more," Chase said, then dropped his head to hers.

Chapter Ten

Sadie closed her eyes and lost herself in Chase's kiss. She'd been so afraid to tell him about how she'd led Jonathan on to stall him, but she shouldn't have worried. She could tell Chase was upset on her behalf, but he wasn't disgusted or turned off by what she'd done.

Thank God.

She opened her eyes when Chase pulled back and she felt his hands at her waist. He was sitting astride her, gently easing the shirt up her belly. She didn't feel one second of angst about her position, even though Jonathan had held her on her back while he'd hurt her. She lifted her arms to assist Chase with her shirt and didn't watch where it went when he threw it off the side of the bed.

His eyes were glued to her chest and there was a slight frown on his face.

She glanced down to see what he was looking at and didn't see anything but her own skin. But she remembered the marks that had been there from the brutal way Jonathan had handled her. They'd lasted for a couple of weeks and had only recently faded away.

She brought her hands up to cover herself, but Chase caught them in his own. He kissed both palms then said, "Don't hide from me, Sparky. Don't ever hide from me. You're beautiful."

Then he blew her mind.

As if he knew exactly where the bruises had been, he leaned over and kissed the phantom marks. He laved her, as if his saliva had the power to further heal her wounds. When he was done, he moved down farther and laid his cheek on her belly. His elbows were cocked out, his hands covering the sides of her tits, his thumbs gently caressing her rock-hard nipples.

She would've thought he was asleep if it wasn't for the movement of his fingers.

"Chase?" she asked after he didn't move for almost a minute. "Is your arm all right? Does it hurt?"

"My arm is fine. I just need a minute," he said softly.

"You okay?" Sadie insisted, worried about him now.

"I want to fucking kill him," Chase said in a low, even tone.

Sadie blinked. Wow. He felt boneless on her, not tense, not even upset. But his words communicated that he was as agitated as she'd ever heard him. She ran her hands over his head, ruffling his brown hair. She loved the feel of him.

"I'm okay," she whispered.

She felt Chase take a deep breath, felt the warm air against the sensitive skin of her belly as he exhaled, then he lifted his head. "I will never hurt you, Sadie. Never."

"I know."

His hands began to move again, kneading and caressing her body. Before long, she was shifting under him, impatient for him to move things forward. "Chase... I need..." Her words trailed off as he took a nipple in his mouth and suckled her gently.

He let go with a popping sound and grinned. "You need what, Sparky? What do you need?"

"You. Naked," she gasped out.

Chase moved until he was kneeling over her, then reached behind his head and grabbed the material of his shirt. He pulled it up and over his head in one smooth movement, tossing it aside when it was off.

Sadie's eyes roamed down his body. He was built. Not as well built as some of the men she'd seen, but to her, he was perfect. He had a slight smattering of dark hair on his chest that tapered down to his happy trail. It led into the waistband of his boxers.

When her eyes went lower, she saw exactly how excited he was to be with her. The bulge in his boxers was so impressive, she figured if he moved in just the right way, his cock would pop out of the slit in the front of the material. Just thinking about what it would look like made her smile.

"Hey, my face is up here," he teased, putting a finger under her chin and forcing her head up so she had to look him in the eyes.

Sadie chuckled and kept her eyes on his even as her hands moved to his body. She ran them up his thighs, skipping over his cock, up his belly to his pecs. She dug her fingers into his skin and smiled wider when he gasped. Then she reversed her movements, running her palms over his chest hair, down to the beautiful *V* muscles, and back to his thighs. She did it again, running her hands all the way up his body, then back down.

Throughout it all, they stared at each other and Chase didn't move, letting her explore.

When her hands started up his body for the third time, he finally caught them in his own and leaned over, holding her arms over her head by the wrists.

"You told me everything, didn't you?" Chase asked in a low voice.

"Everything?"

"Yeah. You didn't forget to tell me he thrust his hand down your pants or that he forced himself on you after all, right?"

"No, I didn't forget, because he didn't. I didn't let him get that far." Sadie wanted to get pissed, but she couldn't bring herself to feel it when Chase was looking at her the way he was. "I might have let him touch my boobs, but there's no way I would've let him go any further."

"I just wanted to be sure you wouldn't have any flashbacks or bad moments when I continue my exploration of your beautiful body."

"I know it's you touching me, Chase. I *want* you to touch me."

Chase groaned. He let go of her hands and eased his way down her body until he was lying between her thighs. He slipped his fingers under the sides of her black cotton panties and, without fuss or fanfare, pulled them down her legs.

Sadie helped to kick them off and promptly forgot about them when she felt Chase's fingers brush over the short curls.

"Fuck. This is so fucking sexy," he said.

Sadie saw he couldn't take his eyes off of her. "What?"

"This. Your red hair here. It's the exact shade as on your head."

Sadie rolled her eyes but didn't disturb Chase as he examined her. When several seconds went by and he hadn't moved on, she asked, "You gonna get on with it anytime soon there, Chase? Or do I need to pleasure myself?" She snaked a hand down her belly to her clit.

Chase caught her wrist and finally looked up. "As much as I would love to see that, Sparky, I'm gonna take a rain check. I've got to taste you." And with that, he settled himself back between her legs and lowered his head.

Sadie jolted at the first touch of his tongue then moaned at the second. His hand came up and he separated her folds and ran the tip of his tongue between them. Groaning, he did it again. And again.

Then he shifted, balanced himself on his elbows, brought his other hand up to hold her open for his mouth, and began to feast. That was the only word she could think of to describe what he was doing to her.

It was amazing and overwhelming at the same time. Sadie wasn't a virgin; she'd been with men before, but this… No one had made her feel the way Chase did. It wasn't his technique, per se—it was the enthusiasm he was using. He wasn't half-heartedly licking her until he felt he'd done it long enough and could get on with fucking her—no, he was devouring her.

Just when she didn't think it could get any better, Chase shifted again. One hand pulled the hood of her clit back so he could have direct access to the small, sensitive nub, and his head dropped.

He covered her clit with his mouth and sucked, hard. Her hips bucked, but he easily held her down as he feasted. Chase's tongue swirled and licked and she'd never felt anything like it. Instead of closing her eyes and losing herself in his touch, she watched him.

For a long moment, all she saw was the top of his head, but as if he could sense her gaze on him, he tilted his head up and their eyes met. His pupils were dilated and she could see his jaw working as he made love to her with his mouth.

"Chase," she whispered.

Her thighs shook and her hips were in constant motion now, bucking under him as her orgasm got closer and closer. Just before she went over the edge, she felt a finger from his other hand slowly push into her soaking-wet sheath, his finger curling as he searched for her G-spot. Sadie had only had one G-spot orgasm in the past, and that was with a lot of trial and error with her trusty, specially-shaped vibrator.

As if he had a map of her body and already knew exactly where to find it, Chase's finger zeroed in on the bumpy spot inside her. He stroked the sensitive bundle of nerves and she jerked, throwing her head back and clutching the sheets at her sides. When he did it again, at the same time sucking hard on her clit, she lost it.

The strongest, most intense orgasm she'd ever had swept through her body, making her softly cry out and arch her back under Chase. He released the suction on her clit for a moment, but then began to lick it…hard.

"Fuck, Chase," Sadie cried as her body was forcefully thrown over the cliff once more. She felt his finger moving inside her but it was as if she were having an out-of-body experience. She was there, but she wasn't.

A sheen of sweat covered her body as she writhed under Chase's expert hands. When she finally felt as if she could breathe again, she opened her eyes. Chase was crouched over her once more. His boxers were gone and she felt the tip of his cock between her legs. Looking down, she saw that he'd covered himself with a condom while she was recovering and was poised to enter her.

"Sadie?" he asked, waiting for her permission.

In response, Sadie dropped her knees to the sides and opened for him. Her hands ran around his waist to his ass and she gripped him. "Yes."

As if the one word was all that had been holding him back, Chase was moving the second she uttered it. His hand gripped the base of his dick and he slowly but steadily pressed inside her.

Even though she was soaking wet, she still felt a twinge of discomfort as he pushed into her body.

But Chase didn't stop until he was in as far as he could go. He moved a hand around to her ass and tugged on one butt cheek, pulling her folds apart a fraction of an inch, and allowing himself one more millimeter of space inside her.

They both sighed at the sensation.

Then he stilled. They stayed frozen like that for a moment, staring into each other's eyes, knowing somehow their lives were forever changed already by the act of him entering her body.

Sadie squirmed under him. The pain had disappeared and, in its wake, she felt full. But she wanted more. Needed more. "Please," she begged.

"What do you need?" Chase ground out between clenched teeth. "Am I hurting you? I saw you wince but I couldn't stop. God help me, I couldn't stop."

"No!" she cried, closing her knees and hugging his hips, terrified he was going to pull out. "It doesn't hurt. It was uncomfortable for a second because it's been a while for me, but please don't stop." She squeezed her inner muscles hard, trying to show him without words how he felt inside her.

He groaned. "Fuck, Sparky. You're going to make me come before I even move inside you. You're so fucking beautiful. I couldn't wait. Feeling you around my finger… Hot. Wet. Damn."

Sadie smiled. He wasn't using complete sentences, as if he was too flustered to be able to think. "Fuck me, Chase. Make yourself feel good."

"Oh, there's no doubt I feel good," he told her as he slowly pulled out until only the tip of his cock was inside her. Then he ever so slowly pushed inside her once more. "No doubt you feel good around me."

He made love to her then. With slow, gentle strokes. He felt good, but Sadie knew she'd never get off if he didn't speed things up. Too shy to tell him what she needed, she moved a hand between her legs and caressed his shaft the next time he pulled out of her body. He groaned and she smiled.

Then she used her wet fingers to caress her clit. She jerked at the first touch, still extremely sensitive from his oral ministrations earlier. But the more she played with herself, the better it felt.

"Fuck, that's hot," Chase said from above her. "How hard can you take it?" he asked.

"As hard as you want to give it to me," Sadie said. Then she overcame her shyness and told him, "It feels good when you go slow, but I can't come that way."

"What do you need?"

"You."

The words were barely out of her mouth when Chase slammed his cock into her body. "Like that?"

"God, yes! More."

Chase didn't say anything else, just shifted his hands to her hips to hold her still, and then he started hammering into her body with punishing thrusts. Sadie could feel her boobs bouncing each time he bottomed out inside her, but she didn't even care. All she could think about was Chase's hard cock powering into her.

She rubbed her fingers faster over her clit. Chase moved his hands to her inner thighs and pressed hard, opening her up to him. The position felt dirty and carnal, and she'd never been made love to this way before.

Chase's hands were strong and firm on her body, moving her legs where he wanted them, where he could see everything he was doing to her.

Her finger moved even faster now, and she was so close to coming. "Fuck me," she murmured again. "I'm almost there."

Happy he hadn't pushed her hand away and tried to manipulate her clit himself—she hated when guys thought they knew her body better than she did—Sadie resisted the urge to close her eyes and kept her gaze glued between her legs, where Chase's cock was pounding into her. His shaft was covered with her excitement and the sounds coming from his thrusts were almost obscene.

The sex was raw. And real. And the most amazing thing she'd ever felt. She roughly fingered her clit and felt her orgasm rapidly approaching. Before she could say a word, it was there. Her whole body shook with the force of her pleasure, enhanced by Chase's brutal thrusts inside her spasming channel.

Just as she was coming down from the heights of rapture, Chase thrust one more time inside her body and grunted. His head was thrown back, his nipples hard as diamonds on his chest. She could tell he held his breath, and Sadie could actually feel his cock twitching rhythmically with each spurt of come from the tip.

When he was finished, Chase gazed down at her with a look of such adoration on his face, Sadie wanted to cry. She would give anything she owned to have him always look at her that way. Without a word, he leaned to the side, taking her with him. They lay with their legs intertwined and their arms around each other for what seemed like hours, but in reality was probably only a few minutes.

Finally, he lifted his head and kissed her. He tasted musky, like her, but Sadie didn't care. She had no thoughts about what the next day would bring. No thoughts about what had previously happened with Jonathan. She could only smell, taste, and see Chase.

"Tired?" he asked softly when he'd pulled his lips from hers.

"Mmmm."

He went to move away from her and Sadie tightened her arms around him. "Where you goin'?"

"I need to take care of this condom, then I was going to check on Fletch."

"Stay?" she asked. "Just for a while?"

He stared into her eyes for a beat, then nodded. "Yeah, for a little bit. Give me a second."

She nodded and watched as he pulled back the covers and padded completely naked to the bathroom. His ass was almost as gorgeous as the rest of him. Within moments he was coming back toward her.

He didn't seem to have an ounce of modesty, as he didn't try to cover himself up or otherwise hide any part of his naked body from her. He slipped back under the covers and took her into his arms.

Sadie sighed in contentment and snuggled into him, getting comfortable.

"For the record," Chase said, "I don't want you to go back up to Dallas. I know that's where your job is and where your aunt and uncle are, but I don't think I can go back to sleeping by myself ever again."

Surprised, Sadie lifted her head. "Are you asking me to move in with you?"

"I don't know," Chase admitted, looking away before bringing his eyes back to hers. "The logical part of my brain says it's too fast. That I'm talking crazy. We need to get to know each other better before we make that kind of commitment. We've basically already lived together for a month, but I was on my best behavior. Once we get comfortable with each other, you might not like that I need to watch the news every morning. That I can't ever remember to put the seat down on the toilet. That I'll totally take advantage of you living with me by letting you do the laundry all the time because I hate doing it.

"But my emotional side is screaming at me to never let you go. To put a ring on your finger so you can't leave me. So every other man who dares to look at you knows you're taken…by me. Hell, I'm even contemplating doing the laundry, dishes, and vacuuming for the rest of my life if you'll have me."

"Chase," Sadie murmured.

"Shhhhh. Just think about it. We don't have to make any decisions right this second. But you should absolutely know that this isn't a fling for me. The second you ran into my arms, freaked way the fuck out but trying hard not to show it—hell, before I even met you, had only seen a picture, I think I knew."

"Knew what?"

"That I wanted you in my life. Under me, over me, next to me. I never believed in love at first sight. Thought my sister was crazy for falling in love with Ghost after a one-night stand. But I get it now."

Sadie's stomach churned with his words. "I thought women were supposed to be the ones who wanted more and the guys were always afraid of commitment," she quipped.

"Apparently, I'm just special," Chase drawled.

Sadie giggled.

"Sleep," Chase ordered again. "If I get up, don't freak. I'm just checking on Fletch and making sure all is well. Okay?"

"Okay. Chase?"

"Yeah, Sparky?"

"I'm glad I'm not the only one who felt that way that night at the school. When you put your arms around me, I finally felt safe. Even when no one could find Jonathan, standing next to you and holding your hand, I knew there was nowhere else I'd rather be."

He didn't reply verbally but tightened his hold around her.

"Chase?"

"You're supposed to be sleeping," he said, the humor easy to hear in his tone.

"I'm also glad one of your friends survived that mission."

"Me too, Sadie. Me too."

"I'd like to meet him someday."

"I'd like that too. Now hush."

"Yes, Sir," she smart-mouthed.

Chase leaned over and kissed her, and they both fell quiet.

Sadie eventually drifted to sleep with Chase's heartbeat echoing in her ear and his words rattling around in her brain. *I don't want you to go back up to Dallas.*

Chapter Eleven

Sadie was woken up sometime later by an earth-shaking *boom*.

She had no idea what time it was. Instantly alarmed, she felt for Chase in the bed next to her, but the sheets were cold. Without thinking, she leaped out of bed and raced to put some clothes on. She pulled on the Army T-shirt of Chase's she'd been wearing earlier and ran into the bathroom to grab her jeans. She shoved her feet into her sneakers and raced to the door.

Just as she opened it, another explosion rocked the house.

She was thrown backward and slammed into the wall across the room, hitting her head before sliding down to the floor. Stunned, she sat there a moment before crawling back toward the bedroom door and peering out into the hallway. There was a lot of dust floating in the air, making her cough as she looked to her right.

The roof above the stairs had collapsed, cutting off one floor of the house from the other.

"Chase?" she called, coughing as more dust got into her lungs.

"Sadie? Is that you?" a feminine voice called from down the hall directly in front of her.

She carefully got to her feet, feeling tender after being thrown backward by the blast. "Emily? Rayne?" Sadie asked.

"It's me. Rayne. Are you okay?"

"I think so," Sadie told her.

Rayne eventually came into view, crawling down the hallway on her hands and knees.

"Where's Emily?"

"I'm here," a voice said from behind Rayne.

Both women turned and saw Emily limping toward them. "Do you have Annie?"

Sadie was somewhat shocked at how well both women were handling the fact that it sounded, and looked, like a bomb had just rocked the house.

"No," Rayne said.

As if on cue, all three women turned to look at Annie's bedroom door—the one closest to the stairs. The doorframe was crooked, the door itself hanging off center. They all raced toward it at the same time.

Sadie helped the others tug at the debris blocking the bedroom door.

"Annie?" Emily yelled.

"Mommy?" the little girl shouted.

Sadie pulled more desperately at the chunks of drywall and wood that were keeping them from Annie. She sounded scared, and it reminded Sadie too much of how the little girls had to have felt at Bexar.

"It's me, baby. Hang on, I'm coming!" Emily told her daughter, obviously trying very hard to keep her composure.

They cleared enough to reveal a small hole in the wall, but no matter what they did, they couldn't remove any more of the debris. Emily carefully lay on the ground and peered through the hole. "Annie? Can you come here?"

"I can't, Mommy," Annie whined. "My leg's stuck under something."

"Shit, why can't Kassie be here?" Rayne muttered. "Or better yet, Bryn…Fish's woman. They're both smaller than we are."

"I can fit," Sadie said with no hesitation. She began to slither through the small hole. The only thought in her head was getting to the little girl, making sure she was safe. To reassure her.

She had the awful suspicion that whatever had happened to the house was undoubtedly Jonathan's doing.

The hole was a tight fit. Sadie felt something dig into the skin on her back as she pressed her way into Annie's room, but she ignored it. A couple scrapes and bruises would go away.

Finally, just when she thought maybe she wouldn't fit after all, her hips popped through the hole and she was in Annie's bedroom.

Crawling on her hands and knees, Sadie made her way over to the bed, the mattress askew.

The little girl wasn't on it.

"Annie?"

"Here!"

Turning, Sadie saw Annie on the other side of the room. Whatever caused the explosion had thrown the child ten feet away from the bed.

Sadie crawled over to the little girl and put her hand on her forehead. Her hair was a tangled mess and her GI Joe pajamas were dirty and torn in places, but Sadie didn't see any major wounds, at least nothing that was bleeding.

"Where do you hurt?" Sadie asked.

"My leg."

Sadie saw that one of the wall studs was lying across the little girl's lower legs, held in place by her dresser.

"How is she?" Emily called from the hole near the door. "Can you get her loose?"

"She's good," Sadie yelled back. "I'm gonna move the piece of furniture off her legs, then use the fire ladder and get her out through the window. It's mostly broken and it'll be easier to get her out that way."

"We'll go back down the hall when you're clear and see if we can't get out the window in the guest room," Rayne said. "We'll meet you at the back of the house. Okay?"

Sadie worked on clearing Annie's legs, and at the same time shouted back, "Okay! Have you heard from the guys?"

There was a long pause before Emily responded. "No. I sent Rayne to yell for them down the stairs. But so far they haven't answered."

Sadie closed her eyes in despair. If any of them were hurt—or God forbid, dead—it would be her fault.

She shouldn't have let Chase talk her into coming here. She knew what Jonathan was like. He liked causing pain. Got off on it.

A light touch on her arm brought her head around, and she stared into Annie's blue eyes. "My daddy's fine. He's a hero."

Her words were said with such conviction, Sadie actually believed her. She smiled. It was a weak effort, but it was more than she would've been capable of a couple of minutes ago. "How about you and me get out of here?" she asked.

Annie nodded, then looked around the room. "Can we bring my Army man? I can't leave without him."

"I don't think—" Sadie began, but Annie interrupted her.

"I need him! I can't leave him behind. He should be fine, he was in his special case my friend gave me. Please, Sadie, please!" Tears poured down Annie's cheeks as she pleaded with her.

For the first time, Sadie heard real panic in the little girl's voice. From all that she'd heard about Annie from Chase, and from what she'd seen the night before, she knew that she wasn't one to freak out. She wasn't a whiny child at all. So for her to be this upset, Sadie knew the doll was important to her.

"Okay, Annie, don't cry. We'll find him and take him with us."

Sadie shoved one more time at the surprisingly heavy dresser and it finally shifted. "Scoot back, Annie. I can't help while I've got hold of this. Pull your legs out. Slowly though, in case something's broken."

Annie did as she was told and pulled her little body out from under the debris. Once she cleared it, Sadie dropped the mangled dresser and went straight to Annie's side. Using the first aid she knew, she felt her legs to make sure they weren't broken. The little girl flinched a couple of times but didn't scream out in pain.

Sighing in relief, Sadie turned her head to the door. "Emily?"

"Yeah! I'm here. What's wrong?"

"Nothing. Annie's free. As far as I can tell, nothing's broken. Go on, meet us outside."

"Thank God," Emily said. "Rayne tried to remove some of the debris at the top of the stairs to get the guys' attention. Ghost finally answered. He says they're okay. Annie?"

"Yeah, Mommy?" Annie answered, her voice stronger now that she knew her precious military doll wasn't going to be left behind.

"Go outside with Sadie. Stay by her side. I mean it. Right by her side. Okay?"

"I will, Mommy. Is Daddy really okay?"

"Of course he is. We'll see him once we get outside."

"Are you scared, Sadie?" Annie asked quietly.

Sadie looked down at the small child. She sounded like someone twice her age at that moment.

"Yeah, baby. A little."

"Being scared means you're about to do something really really brave. Remember, Mommy? You said that to me when we were in the metal box."

Sadie didn't know what Annie was talking about, but she loved her optimistic attitude and how she was trying to comfort her mother.

"I remember, baby. Now, go on. Get outside with Sadie. Your dad and I will be there as soon as we can."

"I love you, Mommy."

"Love you too."

Annie's gaze roamed the room and she pointed in the opposite corner. "There he is!"

Sadie turned toward where Annie was pointing and saw a plastic doll the size of a Barbie inside a protective case. She hurried over and grabbed it, along with a pair of shoes that were miraculously still sitting right where Annie probably left them after taking them off. She brought both the shoes and the doll back to Annie's side.

The little girl hugged her precious doll and beamed up at Sadie.

"Quick, Annie. Put on your shoes and we'll go."

Annie did as ordered, slipping her tennis shoes on without a word. When she was done, she grabbed her Army man and looked up at Sadie. "I'm ready to go now," she announced.

"Go ahead and see if you can stand. We'll go from there."

Annie stood and wobbled for a moment before gaining her equilibrium.

"Does anything hurt?" Sadie asked.

"My head a little, and my legs where they were stucked under the dresser. But I'm okay."

Sadie was constantly amazed at the child. She was scared, but she was holding it together.

Annie clutched her doll with one arm and took Sadie's hand with her free one. They walked over to the destroyed window. Sadie knocked the loose glass out of the way with a piece of wood from the floor and peered out.

It was dark and quiet. Almost eerily so. The loud explosions should've woken up the neighbors, even though they weren't exactly close. The nearest house was about a mile away. Hopefully the police and fire department had already been called.

Sadie shivered. Suddenly, she did not want to leave the house. She knew without a doubt that Jonathan was lying in wait in the darkness. Waiting to snatch her away. He'd take her where no one would ever find her and do horrible things to her. She'd probably end up in a cage in a basement somewhere, having baby after baby that he'd take from her the second they cleared her womb.

"Sadie?" Annie asked in a small voice next to her. "Aren't we leaving? I wanna leave."

"Yeah, baby, we're going," Sadie reassured the seven-year-old. She unfolded the rope ladder that was lying under the window. "Stay here while I climb out. Once I make sure it's safe, I'll help you."

Carefully, Sadie stepped over the ledge of the window and climbed down the ladder. Once she was outside, she looked around once again. She couldn't see much from where she was standing near the back porch, but a quick peek around one corner revealed orange flames wrapping around the side of the house to the front.

She hadn't realized there was a fire. Refusing to panic and blocking out everything but making sure Annie was safe, Sadie called out for the little girl.

"Catch, Sadie!" Annie yelled from above.

Luckily Sadie was paying attention, because without any other warning, Annie had dropped the plastic case with her Army doll inside. She caught it and immediately put it on the ground. Sadie didn't bitch at the girl for her actions. The sooner the doll was safe, the sooner Annie would follow.

And she did. Within seconds, Annie had shimmied down the rope ladder and was in her arms. Sadie clasped the little girl to her chest and sighed in relief. Awkwardly, not wanting to put Annie down, she leaned over and grabbed the doll. Annie held the box under one arm, the other staying around Sadie's neck.

Not knowing where to go, and seeing no sign yet of Emily or Rayne, Sadie shifted away from the side of the house that was on fire. Once they rounded the opposite back corner, Sadie saw that the garage was intact. Ironic, really. She and Chase had stayed in the main house to be safe. Although, she realized that Jonathan must have known exactly where she was. If she and Chase had been in the garage, she had no doubt *it* would currently be burning right now.

She stood with Annie at the back corner of the house, keeping an eye out for the women who were supposed to be meeting them. As the seconds ticked by, Sadie felt more alone than she ever had before. Jonathan wasn't going to give up. He'd destroy whatever he had to, hurt whoever he had to, in order to get his hands on her. The oppressive weight of the danger she was in, and the danger in which she'd put everyone around her, threatened to strangle her.

"Look! Someone's here!" Annie said suddenly, pointing.

Sadie forced herself to pay attention, turned to where Annie was indicating. Sure enough, there was a set of headlights coming down the long driveway at a high rate of speed. She shielded her eyes from the bright lights and when she got a good glimpse of the car, Sadie wanted to both laugh and cry.

She should've known her uncle wouldn't wait until a normal time in the morning to show up. He probably thought about waiting, but decided he'd come down tonight, just in case, and Ian could come in the morning as usual. Thank God he decided not to wait.

Sadie would've recognized his car anywhere. He loved that 1972 Scout. It resembled a Bronco, but in a retro way. It was a hardtop convertible, and Sadie knew Sean had put in a lot of hours making it perfect.

The relief she felt that her uncle had arrived almost brought her to her knees. Instead, she ran with Annie to meet him—just reaching the front of Fletch's home when there was yet another loud *boom*, causing Annie to yelp in surprise.

And Sadie watched in horror as a fireball came out of the woods beyond the far side of the house, straight toward her uncle's car.

She screamed "No!" as whatever it was hit the back of the Scout and flipped it.

The car rolled several times and ended up lying on its roof next to the garage. She saw movement inside, and her hope rose that since whatever had hit the car had only grazed the back end, maybe Sean was all right.

"Oh my gosh," Annie said softly. "Who's that?"

Sadie turned her attention from the wreckage. Her head couldn't keep up with what was happening. She looked to where Annie was pointing and gasped. A man was walking toward them. She could make out a smirk on his face in the light coming from the fire at the house.

Jonathan.

She should've been scared. She should've been freaking out. But suddenly, Sadie was just mad. *Furious.* How dare he blow up Fletch's house? How dare he try to kill her uncle? How *dare* he scare Emily, Rayne, and Annie? He had no right. *No* right.

Quickly, she leaned over and put Annie's feet on the ground. She turned the little girl and pushed her in the opposite direction from where Jonathan was slowly and steadily sauntering toward them. It was obvious he thought he had all the time in the world to get to her. Asshole.

"Run, Annie! Go through the trees to your neighbor's house. No matter what you hear, don't stop. Understand?"

Annie immediately nodded, then turned on her heel and ran into the woods. She was limping a little, but she soldiered on.

Without looking at Jonathan again, Sadie ran toward her uncle's car. She wasn't going to docilely be kidnapped. Nope. She had no idea where Chase was or if he was injured. If he wasn't, she knew without a doubt he'd do everything in his power to make sure she was safe.

But first she had to help herself…and that meant getting her uncle out of his wrecked car.

Chapter Twelve

Chase coughed and tried his best not to pass out. He'd been talking to Ghost and Fletch in the living room about the plan for the morning once Sadie's uncle arrived, when the world around them had exploded. One minute they'd been standing there, and the next he was lying on the ground trying to catch his breath.

He sat up, momentarily confused, but quickly figured out they were under attack when he saw the hole in the side of the house and Ghost and Fletch lying motionless across from him.

His first thought was for Sadie, but from what he could tell, the missile, or whatever it was that had come through the house, had hit the side opposite the upstairs bedrooms. He turned his head to look toward the stairs and gasped in horror when he saw they were cut off by a pile of debris.

Fletch moaned then, and Chase turned his attention from the blocked stairs to his friends. He crawled over to Fletch, wincing with every movement. His side hurt, bad, but he ignored it for the moment.

"Fletch, wake up, man."

Fletch's eyes opened then closed again. Chase saw a large piece of wood sticking out of his side. He was bleeding profusely. Swearing, he looked over to Ghost. The other man was sitting up now and shaking his head as if trying to get his bearings.

"Ghost, Fletch is hurt," Chase told him. "I need your help."

As if his words were a switch, Ghost turned his head and immediately crawled over to where Chase was kneeling over Fletch. "Shit. That doesn't look good."

"I know, but we've got to get that out."

"Fuck." Ghost looked around as if searching for something. "We'd be better off leaving it in place, but I don't think we've got a choice. We need to stop that bleeding."

"Right, that's what I was thinking," Chase agreed. "If he wasn't bleeding so heavily, we could leave it in, but if we don't stop the blood, he'll bleed out before help can get here."

Ghost nodded grimly and quickly took off his T-shirt.

Chase reached for the wood. "I'll pull, you get ready to apply pressure. Ready? One, two, *three!*" On the last count, Chase pulled and the wood easily slid out of Fletch's side. He moaned but didn't open his eyes.

Ghost was there to immediately apply pressure to the hole in his teammate's side. Using his T-shirt to help staunch the blood flow, he leaned on the wound and turned to Chase. "The women?"

"Not sure. The stairway is blocked, but it looks like this room took the brunt of the damage."

Ghost turned to look at the stairs. "Fuck. Jonathan?"

"That's my assumption," Chase agreed.

"*Fuck,*" Ghost repeated.

"My guess is that he's trying to force us out of the house. Cutting us off from the women was just a bonus. He's not going to try to face us one-on-one. He's perfectly happy working from a distance and doing a snatch-and-grab."

"Ghost?" Rayne's muffled voice came from above the blocked stairway.

"Yeah, baby, I'm here," Ghost replied in a loud voice.

"Are you okay?"

"How are you? And the others?"

Chase noted that he didn't tell Rayne about Fletch.

"We're good. We can't get in Annie's room, but Sadie somehow wiggled in there through a hole the size of a dime. I smell smoke... Is there a fire in there?"

Chase turned to look and saw that indeed there was a fire. He'd been so intent on Fletch that he hadn't even noticed. He coughed.

"Yeah, but we're good. We're gettin' out now."

"Ghost?" Rayne asked. "Where's Fletch?"

"He's here," Ghost told her. Then added, "He's hurt, Rayne, but he's gonna be fine. Me and Chase have him. Hear me? He's good. You guys just need to get outside. But stay together. Under no circumstances should you split up."

"We can't get to Annie! Sadie said she's going to take her out the window in her room."

Chase swore under his breath. He and Ghost looked down at Fletch. They were both needed to get him out of the house. Ghost couldn't take his hands off the wound, and he couldn't carry him and keep pressure on his side at the same time.

Ghost obviously came to the same conclusion because he told Rayne, "Get out of the house. Find Sadie and stick with her. This wasn't an accident. You hear me?"

"Oh God. Yeah, Ghost, I hear you."

Both he and Ghost heard Rayne calling out to Emily as she backed away from the blocked entryway. "Come on, Em. We need to get out of here. Sadie's waiting for us. I'm sure Annie's fine. She's probably excited about all this, not scared. Come on." Her voice shook, but she was doing what Ghost had asked.

Chase met Ghost's eyes. They both coughed as the room continued to fill with smoke. The flames were higher now. They didn't have a choice; they couldn't stay here, no matter how dangerous it could be to move Fletch. They were damned if they did and damned if they didn't. But the fire would kill them all if they didn't get out of the house.

"I'll go recon a way out," Chase told Ghost.

He nodded.

Chase rose on wobbly legs and put a hand on his side as he stood up. It hurt like a motherfucker. He looked down at his hand and saw it was smeared with blood. It wasn't as bad as Fletch's wound, but he'd obviously been hit by flying debris.

The easiest way out would be through the hole in the wall that had been created when the rocket entered the house, but the fire was blocking that exit. He didn't want to use the front door, as they would be sitting ducks by walking into the yard from such an exposed exit. That left the back door that led to the backyard and porch area.

Chase peered through the curtain and tried to assess the danger. He couldn't see much, as it was still dark, but there didn't seem to be anything blocking the door and preventing their exit. They could get Fletch out and into the tall grass surrounding the backyard. Then he could go and find Sadie and the others.

He made his way back to Fletch and Ghost, coughing the whole time. The smoke was getting thick, and soon Chase knew they wouldn't be able to see anything. He gestured toward the back door and Ghost nodded. Chase grabbed hold of Fletch's arm on the side that wasn't injured and raised his eyebrows at Ghost, asking if he was ready.

When Ghost nodded, Chase used all his strength to pull Fletch across the floor by his arm. Ghost stayed right by their side, on his knees, keeping pressure on Fletch's wound as they made their way toward the exit.

The amount of effort it took to drag the unconscious man was enormous, and Chase felt blood dripping from his side. But he wasn't going to give up. Fletch had allowed him to stay at his house, and now it had been destroyed by the very person they'd been trying to stay hidden from.

He vowed right then and there to make sure the man was compensated every penny it would take to rebuild his house. The FBI would most certainly pitch in, if not outright pay for everything. They were desperately trying to find Jonathan, almost as desperate as Chase had been. The stashed weapons in the secret tunnel at the school had made finding Jonathan a priority…and it looked like they'd had a reason to be worried. He obviously hadn't left all of the weapons behind when he'd disappeared. Chase would pull whatever strings it took to get compensation for Fletch.

They reached the back door and Chase checked it one more time. He didn't see anything. He pulled open the door and listened. All he could hear was the crackling of the flames. He nodded at Ghost once more and they worked together to get Fletch outside and across the yard. Pulling the man through the grass was a lot tougher than across the wood floors in his home, but Chase dug deep and managed.

He pulled his friend into the tall grass and panted when they finally stopped. "Someone had to have heard the explosion and called the cops by now. I'll go and get the women and bring them back here," Chase told Ghost.

Just then, a huge explosion sounded from the front of the house.

Both men's heads swung around, even though they couldn't see anything from behind the house.

Ghost's gaze went to something beyond Chase, and he exclaimed, "What the fuck?"

Chase turned in time to see a small shape running away from the house and into the woods as if the hounds of hell were at her heels. She was limping as she ran, but Annie definitely had a destination in mind.

"Dammit," Chase said, wanting to yell out to the little girl, but not willing to risk giving away their position. Fletch was still vulnerable, and Ghost couldn't exactly fight someone off...not with him literally holding Fletch's life in the palms of his hands. Their hands were tied, and Chase was the only one who could freely move at the moment.

"Go," Ghost ordered. "Fuck, *go!*"

Chase didn't stick around to debate the issue. Bent over in a crouch to stay low, he took off for the side of the house. He almost ran right into Rayne and Emily. He grabbed Rayne by the shoulders to keep himself from falling over. "Ghost and Fletch are out back in the tall grass. Go."

"But you're bleeding!" Rayne said with wide eyes. "Bro, you need to come with us." She tugged at his sleeve, not letting go, and looking up at him with such concern and fright, he wanted to scoop her up and tell her that everything was fine. But he didn't have time.

"Annie? Is she with them?" Emily asked urgently.

"No, but she's fine. I saw her myself. She's headed for the neighbor's house. Go. *Please.*"

Without a word, Emily took off running across the yard in the direction Chase said he'd seen her go.

Chase stared at his sister. Her eyes were wide and she had dirt smeared across her forehead. "Go, sis. I got this."

She took a deep breath, then nodded. "Okay, but if you die, I'll never forgive you." And with that, she turned and fled across the yard toward where he'd left Ghost and Fletch.

Chase wanted to smile at his sister's words but couldn't. His side hurt like a bitch, he was starting to feel dizzy from blood loss, and the woman he loved was in danger. He knew it as easily as he knew his own name.

He peeked around the corner of the house—and was on the move before his brain told his feet to move.

Sadie was kneeling next to a car up against the garage. It was lying upside down and the back end had flames coming from it. She was tugging at someone's arm, trying to pull them out of the wreckage.

But that wasn't what had him running after her as fast as he could go. It was the man walking up behind her. Jonathan.

Chase had known all along Jonathan had been behind whatever had hit the house, but seeing him there, walking toward the woman he loved as if he didn't have a care in the world, flipped a switch inside Chase. After hearing what the man had already done to Sadie, there was no way he was going to let him get his hands on her again. No fucking way.

When he got close enough, Chase could hear Sadie saying, "Uncle Sean, are you all right?" as she tugged on his arm, trying to pull him free of the wreckage. He was conscious, and the swear words coming from his mouth would've impressed Chase if he wasn't focused on Jonathan.

"Sadie, look out!" Sean said, but it was too late.

Jonathan walked up behind her and easily pulled her away from the car and her uncle.

Without thinking, Chase didn't even slow down. No one had seen him yet, and he used that to his advantage. He plowed right into Jonathan's side.

All three of them went flying, and Chase did his best to keep from falling on top of Sadie.

They landed in the dirt with loud thumps and Chase's vision went dark briefly when he landed right on his injured side. His hesitation when they fell was enough for Jonathan to get the upper hand.

He rolled and straddled Chase. Both hands went to Chase's throat and he squeezed.

"She's *mine*," Jonathan hissed. "You can't have her!"

Chase tried to gasp for air, but he couldn't get any. The hands around his throat were too tight. He bucked under the other man, but nothing he did made any difference. His side no longer hurt, in fact he didn't feel much of anything. The need for oxygen overrode everything but the sight of the woman he loved more than life itself.

He saw her struggle to stand behind Jonathan.

Refusing to look into the blue eyes filled with hate above him, he kept his eyes on Sadie. She looked like a Valkyrie. Her red hair swirled around her head as if it had a mind of its own. Her hazel eyes sparked with determination. He lost sight of her for a moment, but as soon as he began to panic, she reappeared.

Chase watched with huge eyes as she lifted something above her head.

She brought it down swiftly on Jonathan's back and he immediately let go of Chase's throat.

Chase rolled to the side, away from the man who was trying to kill him, and told his limbs to move. To do something to protect Sadie…

But he didn't need to worry. Sean Taggart rose from the wrecked car next to his niece. He took what Chase could now see was a tire iron from Sadie, and as Jonathan started to stand, Sean swung the iron rod like a baseball bat.

Jonathan's head literally exploded from the impact.

No one said a word for long seconds. Then Sadie cried, "Chase!"

Chase's head thunked back onto the ground and he stared up at the clear night sky, trying to catch his breath. For some reason, he couldn't. Even though Jonathan no longer had hold of his throat, he couldn't get air into his lungs.

Sadie's face appeared above his, her red hair brushing against his cheek. "Chase?"

"I love you," Chase gasped. It was the only thing he could think to say. He hadn't told her earlier, but at that moment, lying on the ground, he knew.

"Oh my God, Chase!" Sadie repeated. Her hand came to rest on his cheek, and Chase tried to smile at her. He loved her touch. His eyes closed.

"No, Chase! Don't close your eyes!" Sadie said desperately.

He opened his eyes and looked up into the panicked ones of the woman he loved. "Say it back," he demanded.

She shook her head. "No. Not now. When you're better. You have to hang on if you want to hear me say it."

Chase's brows furrowed. He needed to hear the words from her mouth. He knew he was dying. He couldn't breathe and something was seriously wrong with his side. He hadn't gotten a good look at it, but it was bad. He knew. "Please," he begged, breathlessly.

Tears coursed down Sadie's face, but she stubbornly shook her head. "*No*. You fight to stay with me and I'll say the words every day for the rest of our lives!"

Chase heard a commotion off to his side but didn't take his eyes off of Sadie's. Everything was fading away, but still he couldn't tear his gaze from hers. Her eyes looked even more beautiful highlighted by her tears. "Jonathan won't hurt you again."

"I know, you saved me," Sadie said.

She moved from his side to the top of his head, and he arched his neck to keep his eyes on hers. He vaguely heard people talking above him but didn't understand what they were saying. Someone was pulling at his shirt, but again, all his focus was on Sadie.

"I love you," he repeated in a croak. "I'd do anything to keep you safe."

"Then fight for me," was her response. "Don't give up!"

Chase opened his mouth to answer, but the darkness creeping in from the sides of his eyes was too much to fight. The last thing he remembered as the blackness overcame him was the sound of sirens in the distance.

He relaxed. The cavalry was coming. Sadie would finally be safe.

* * * *

Later—he had no idea how much time had passed—Chase's eyes opened into slits. Everything hurt, he couldn't move, and he was confused as hell. But the second his eyes opened, Sadie's face came into view.

"Chase?"

He opened his lips but nothing came out. They were too dry and he didn't have an ounce of spit in his mouth.

"I love you."

Sadie's words settled into his soul.

"You hear me, Chase? I love you. You kept your end of the bargain. Your heart stopped twice in surgery, but you didn't give up. I love you. I think I have since the second I crashed into you at Bexar."

Chase stared up into the hazel eyes he loved more than anything on this earth. He opened his mouth once more, to try to tell Sadie that she was his reason for living. That he'd fight the devil himself if it meant he got to come back to her, but before he could do more than croak, her lips were on his.

It was a short kiss. Dry. Merely a touch of her lips to his. But it was the best kiss he'd had in his life.

She pulled back and rested her palm on his chest. "Sleep, Chase. I'll be here when you wake up. I love you."

His eyelids shut, and with her words echoing in his brain, he did as she ordered and slept.

Epilogue

Chase leaned heavily against the wall and simply watched Sadie. She was in his kitchen putting dishes away. She'd taken over as if she'd always lived there. She'd been a godsend, not only helping to take care of him after he'd gotten out of the hospital, but taking care of the everyday things that he couldn't because of his injury.

He'd missed everything that happened after he'd passed out on the ground outside Fletch's house.

The cops, firefighters, and EMTs had shown up en masse. They'd put the fire out fairly quickly, and surprisingly, the house wasn't a complete loss. It would take a lot of work to make it livable again, but much of it could be salvaged.

Annie and Emily had run almost a mile to the neighbor's house, Annie carrying her Army man the entire way, then insisted the neighbors bring them right back after they'd called for help.

Fletch had gone through surgery and was currently recovering, just as Chase was. Fletch's liver had been nicked by the piece of wood and if it hadn't been for Ghost's constant pressure, he would've died out there in the grass.

Sean Taggart had suffered a pretty good gash on his head from hitting the steering wheel, but considering his old car didn't have airbags, he was in remarkably good shape. The Scout was sturdy as hell and the frame had held up remarkably well under the circumstances. Unfortunately, although the car had held together well enough to save Sean's life, the classic vehicle was toast.

Ian was supposed to arrive with Sean, but had gotten held up because he was wrapped up in a situation with one of the bodyguards from McKay-Taggart. That had actually turned out to be a good thing because the passenger side of Sean's Scout had taken the brunt of the damage from the RPG.

Jonathan was most definitely dead. The Feds weren't happy, as they had wanted to interrogate him, but Sean hadn't hesitated to do what he'd needed to do to make sure his niece was safe from any future threat.

The fact that Jonathan had done what he had wasn't exactly a surprise, but everyone was still wondering why. Chase thought he understood, after talking with Sadie, but it wasn't his story to tell.

Jonathan had taken a few rocket-propelled grenades with him the last time he'd escaped from Bexar. He'd shot one into Fletch's house, then a second just moments later, while Chase and the other men were passed out, which was the hit that separated them from the women. He'd used a third on Sean's car—and no one had any doubt the man would've used the fourth RPG the cops had found hidden in the trees near Fletch's house, if he'd had to.

Of course, the government was now trying to figure out where Jonathan's father, Jeremiah Jones, had gotten the weapons in the first place. No one wanted that kind of firepower on the streets.

As for Sadie... She hadn't left his side since he'd almost died on the operating table.

Chase had been hit by a nail. It was a freak accident. The metal missile had embedded itself inside his body and he hadn't even known it. The doctors had said it wouldn't have been so bad, but with the effort he'd put into moving Fletch, then tackling Jonathan, it had moved inside his abdomen, tearing into his large intestine, kidney, and bladder in the process. He'd almost died of both internal bleeding and from the toxins in his body contaminating itself.

Rayne had been by his side almost as much as Sadie, and he'd finally had to kick her out of his room. When she refused to leave, he'd sicced Ghost on her. He loved that his sister was concerned about him, but he was going to be fine.

Sean Taggart had hung around for a week and had been joined by his wife, Grace. They'd wanted to make sure their niece was all right after everything that had happened. Chase actually owed both of them a huge debt of gratitude. Sean had helped Sadie rent the large apartment near the Army post—and move all of his belongings out of his old apartment and into the new one before he was discharged from the hospital.

It was a ground-floor unit so he didn't have to do stairs.

He and Sean had had a long talk late one night. The older man had wanted to know what his intentions were toward his niece. Chase had no problem looking the notorious man in the eye and telling him how much he loved Sadie and wanted to marry her.

As Chase stood against the wall, watching Sadie putter around in their kitchen, he momentarily closed his eyes in gratitude for all he had. He would heal, and he'd be able to rejoin his unit soon. Sadie was living with him and they shared a bed every night. She'd officially quit her job at McKay-Taggart up in Dallas and was currently looking for a job in the Fort Hood area.

"Chase?" came her soft voice.

When he opened his eyes, she was standing right next to him with a hand on his biceps.

"I'm good," he reassured her.

"You sure?"

"I'm sure. But I do have something I need to tell you."

"What?"

Chase hated that Sadie looked freaked, so he quickly said, "I was wrong."

Her brow crinkled. "About what?"

"About women being in combat. You were right. Women are just as capable. I was being hardheaded and sexist. If you hadn't been there…" His voice trailed off as he struggled to contain his emotions.

Sadie didn't gloat or even say "I told you so." She simply squeezed his arm in support.

Chase cleared his throat and continued his thought. "I think Rayne being in the middle of that coup in Egypt really screwed with my head. Not to mention that I've been hanging out with the Delta teams. I promise to be better at not jumping to sexist conclusions."

"Thank you. I've been in the unique position of watching all the operatives at McKay-Taggart in action…men *and* women. I've seen what they can do, and how capable they are, firsthand."

"You think, if I asked nicely, Ian would let me come up and train with him and his operatives sometime?" Chase asked.

"Are you serious?" Sadie asked.

"Of course."

"I think they'd love that. They'd love to get the chance to kick your ass."

Chase smiled at Sadie. He felt better after getting that off his chest, but now he had something else he wanted to ask her. He had decided he was going to wait to do this until a more appropriate time, but he couldn't wait one more second.

"I was mad at you when you refused to tell me you loved me. I knew I was probably dying, and I couldn't believe you wouldn't grant me that one last wish." Chase hated the tears that filled her eyes, but he pressed on. "I haven't told anyone this, but I had a dream when I was on the operating table. I don't know that that's even the right word, but whatever. Anyway, I was in a field of sunflowers. They were all taller than my head and I couldn't see anything. I kept calling for you, but you weren't answering. I thought that Jonathan had gotten to you. That I hadn't protected you.

"Then I heard you. Your voice was faint, but you kept asking me to come back to you. That you wanted to tell me something. I yelled and screamed that I was there. That I was coming, but you couldn't hear me. I started walking toward your voice, determined to get to you. The sunflowers turned into hands grabbing at me, trying to keep me from you, but I refused to let them hold me back. The only thing going through my head was getting to you so you could tell me whatever it was that you needed to say. The next thing I knew, I was waking up and you were standing over me.

"You were right, Sparky. Right not to tell me. To make me wait. I'm not saying I wouldn't have fought to get back to you if you'd said it before, I truly believe I would've, but it helped. Gave me something else to fight for. I love you. I'll be the first to admit that I didn't understand Ghost's obsession with my sister, but I get it now. I would do anything for you. *Will* do anything for you."

Chase tried to ignore the tears dripping down Sadie's face as he carefully lowered to one knee in front of her.

She gasped. "Get up, Chase! You're still healing!"

She apparently hadn't figured out what he was doing yet. "I love you, Sadie Jennings. With all that I am. I want to spend the rest of my life with you. I want to be by your side when you have our babies. I want to grow old with you and sit on rocking chairs watching our grandchildren together. I'm going to stay in the Army as long as possible. I love it. But I swear to you right now, I'll do my best to be there when you need me, no matter what. Being an Army wife isn't the easiest job in the world, but you're the strongest woman I've ever met. I would be honored and humbled if you'd agree to spend the rest of your life with me. Will you marry me?"

Sadie stood there a moment, staring down at him with her mouth open, but within seconds of the last word leaving his mouth, she was on her knees too, nodding frantically. "Yes, Chase! Of course, yes! I love you. So much, you'll never know how hard it was *not* to tell you when you were lying in the dirt."

She flung her arms around him, and while her actions made a twinge of pain shoot through his body, he didn't even care. He smiled and leaned back to take her face in his hands. "I don't have a ring yet; I thought I'd let you help me pick one out that you like. I want nothing more than to take you into our bedroom and have we-just-got-engaged sex, but I'm not up for that quite yet. I didn't want to wait though. I love you, Sadie. I know what you're giving up…a job with McKay-Taggart, your life in Dallas. I won't take that for granted."

"I can get another job, and Sean and the others aren't going anywhere. I can still see him and my aunt Grace whenever I want. And sex can wait. Although I do expect you to make it up to me later."

Chase grinned. "Absolutely. Can I ask something else?"

"Of course," she said immediately.

"Do you think you can help me up off the floor?"

She giggled and immediately stood. She held out her hand and Chase took it with a smile. He knew without a doubt Sadie Jennings, soon to be Jackson, would always be there to lend a helping hand, just like he'd be there for her.

* * *

Dear Reader,

If this is the first book you've read by me, I hope you enjoyed it! You can spend more time with the characters you were introduced to in this story—and many others—in both my Delta Force Heroes and my Badge of Honor series.

Learn more about Sadie and Milena, and how they first crossed paths with Jonathan and Jeremiah Jones, in JUSTICE FOR MILENA. Sadie's trip to visit her old friend turns deadly when they unknowingly become the focus of a madman's revenge—and Sadie becomes the object of Jonathan's obsession.

For some quality time with Ghost & Rayne, or Emily, Fletch & precocious little Annie, start with RESCUING RAYNE (which is FREE!), and then try RESCUING EMILY. I hope you'll get as much enjoyment out of reading their stories as I did writing them!

I am forever grateful to Lexi Blake for letting me write Sadie's story. She's an amazing character, and I wish I could be just as tough as she was under those circumstances.

I also want to thank the beautiful people at 1001 Dark Nights. They are amazing to work with, and I'm blessed to have been given the opportunity to be a part of the 1001 DN family.

* * * *

Connect with Susan Online:

Susan's Facebook Profile and Page:
www.facebook.com/authorsstoker
www.facebook.com/authorsusanstoker

Follow Susan on Twitter:
www.twitter.com/Susan_Stoker

Find Susan's Books on Goodreads
www.goodreads.com/SusanStoker

Email: Susan@StokerAces.com

Website: http://www.stokeraces.com/

Sign up for the 1001 Dark Nights Newsletter
and be entered to win a Tiffany Lock necklace.

There's a contest every quarter!

Go to www.1001DarkNights.com for more information.

As a bonus, all subscribers will receive a free copy of
Discovery Bundle Three
Featuring stories by
Sidney Bristol, Darcy Burke, T. Gephart
Stacey Kennedy, Adriana Locke
JB Salsbury, and Erika Wilde

Discover the Lexi Blake Crossover Collection
Available now!

Close Cover by Lexi Blake

Remy Guidry doesn't do relationships. He tried the marriage thing once, back in Louisiana, and learned the hard way that all he really needs in life is a cold beer, some good friends, and the occasional hookup. His job as a bodyguard with McKay-Taggart gives him purpose and lovely perks, like access to Sanctum. The last thing he needs in his life is a woman with stars in her eyes and babies in her future.

Lisa Daley's life is finally going in the right direction. She has finally graduated from college after years of putting herself through school. She's got a new job at an accounting firm and she's finished her Sanctum training. Finally on her own and having fun, her life seems pretty perfect. Except she's lonely and the one man she wants won't give her a second look.

There is one other little glitch. Apparently, her new firm is really a front for the mob and now they want her dead. Assassins can really ruin a fun girls' night out. Suddenly strapped to the very same six-foot-five-inch hunk of a bodyguard who makes her heart pound, Lisa can't decide if this situation is a blessing or a curse.

As the mob closes in, Remy takes his tempting new charge back to the safest place he knows—his home in the bayou. Surrounded by his past, he can't help wondering if Lisa is his future. To answer that question, he just has to keep her alive.

* * * *

Her Guardian Angel by Larissa Ione

After a difficult childhood and a turbulent stint in the military, Declan Burke finally got his act together. Now he's a battle-hardened professional bodyguard who takes his job at McKay-Taggart seriously and his playtime – and his play*mates* – just as seriously. One thing he never does, however, is mix business with pleasure. But when the mysterious, gorgeous Suzanne D'Angelo needs his protection from a stalker, his desire for her burns out of control, tempting him to break all the rules…even as he's drawn into a dark, dangerous world he didn't know existed.

Suzanne is an earthbound angel on her critical first mission: protecting Declan from an emerging supernatural threat at all costs. To keep him close, she hires him as her bodyguard. It doesn't take long for her to realize that she's in over her head, defenseless against this devastatingly sexy human who makes her crave his forbidden touch.

Together they'll have to draw on every ounce of their collective training to resist each other as the enemy closes in, but soon it becomes apparent that nothing could have prepared them for the menace to their lives…or their hearts.

* * * *

Justify Me by J. Kenner

McKay-Taggart operative Riley Blade has no intention of returning to Los Angeles after his brief stint as a consultant on mega-star Lyle Tarpin's latest action flick. Not even for Natasha Black, Tarpin's sexy personal assistant who'd gotten under his skin. Why would he, when Tasha made it absolutely clear that—attraction or not—she wasn't interested in a fling, much less a relationship.

But when Riley learns that someone is stalking her, he races to her side. Determined to not only protect her, but to convince her that—no matter what has hurt her in the past—he's not only going to fight for her, he's going to win her heart. Forever.

* * * *

Say You Won't Let Go by Corinne Michaels

I've had two goals my entire life:
1. Make it big in country music.
2. Get the hell out of Bell Buckle.

I was doing it. I was on my way, until Cooper Townsend landed backstage at my show in Dallas.

This gorgeous, rugged, man of few words was one cowboy I couldn't afford to let distract me. But with his slow smile and rough hands, I just couldn't keep away.

Now, there are outside forces conspiring against us. Maybe we should've known better? Maybe not. Even with the protection from Wade Rycroft, bodyguard for McKay-Taggart, I still don't feel safe. I won't let him get hurt because of me. All I know is that I want to hold on, but know the right thing to do is to let go…

* * * *

His to Protect by Carly Phillips

Talia Shaw has spent her adult life working as a scientist for a big pharmaceutical company. She's focused on saving lives, not living life. When her lab is broken into and it's clear someone is after the top secret formula she's working on, she turns to the one man she can trust. The same irresistible man she turned away years earlier because she was too young and naive to believe a sexy guy like Shane Landon could want *her*.

Shane Landon's bodyguard work for McKay-Taggart is the one thing that brings him satisfaction in his life. Relationships come in second to the job. Always. Then little brainiac Talia Shaw shows up in his backyard, frightened and on the run, and his world is turned upside down. And not just because she's found him naked in his outdoor shower, either.

With Talia's life in danger, Shane has to get her out of town and to her eccentric, hermit mentor who has the final piece of the formula she's been working on, while keeping her safe from the men who are after her. Guarding Talia's body certainly isn't any hardship, but he never expects to fall hard and fast for his best friend's little sister and the only woman who's ever really gotten under his skin.

* * * *

Rescuing Sadie by Susan Stoker

Sadie Jennings was used to being protected. As the niece of Sean Taggart, and the receptionist at McKay-Taggart Group, she was constantly surrounded by Alpha men more than capable, and willing, to lay down their life for her. But when she visits her friend in San Antonio, and acts on suspicious activity at Milena's workplace, Sadie puts both of them in the crosshairs of a madman. After several harrowing weeks, her friend is now safe, but for Sadie, the repercussions of her rash act linger on.

Chase Jackson, no stranger to dangerous situations as a captain in the US Army, has volunteered himself as Sadie's bodyguard. He fell head over heels for the beautiful woman the first time he laid eyes on her. With a Delta Force team at his back, he reassures the Taggart's that Sadie will be safe. But when the situation in San Antonio catches up with her, Chase has to use everything he's learned over his career to keep his promise...and to keep Sadie alive long enough to officially make her his.

About Susan Stoker

New York Times, *USA Today*, and *Wall Street Journal* Bestselling Author Susan Stoker has a heart as big as the state of Tennessee where she lives, but this all-American girl has also spent the last fourteen years living in Missouri, California, Colorado, Indiana, and Texas. She's married to a retired Army man who now gets to follow *her* around the country.

She debuted her first series in 2014 and quickly followed that up with the SEAL of Protection series, which solidified her love of writing and creating stories readers can get lost in.

If you enjoyed this book, or any book, please consider leaving a review. It's appreciated by authors more than you'll know.

* * * *

To sign up for Susan's Newsletter go to:
www.StokerAces.com/contact.html
Or text: STOKER to 24587 for text alerts on your mobile device

Justice for Milena
Badge of Honor: Texas Heroes Book 10
By Susan Stoker
Now Available

Read more about Sadie and how Jonathan got obsessed with her in Justice for Milena.

It's been years since Milena Reinhardt has seen TJ "Rock" Rockwell. The last time, he was nearly a shell of a man…but he was her man…and he tore her heart out of her chest. Circumstances unbeknownst to TJ have ensured Milena's never fully recovered.

TJ left his sniper days behind—for the most part—when he left the Army and become a respected Texas Highway Patrolman. He also left behind Milena. He's convinced it was the right thing to do at the time, but that doesn't mean he's ever forgotten the woman who loved him in his greatest time of need…or has stopped thinking of her since.

Neither thought they'd see each other again, until a pedophile's operation is taken down and the evil man sets his vengeful sights on Milena. This could be their second chance, even though TJ and Milena have enough secrets and trust issues to end any relationship before it starts. But when the bad guy closes in, they'll have to set aside their fears and trust in each other, to save the one thing that means the world to them both.

** Justice for Milena is the 10th book in the Badge of Honor: Texas Heroes Series. Each book is a stand-alone, with no cliffhanger endings.

* * * *

"And did you?" Sadie asked.

"Did I what?" Milena repeated, not sure what they were talking about as she'd gotten lost in memories of TJ.

"Fall at his feet?"

"Of course not!" Milena said quickly—maybe a bit *too* quickly.

"But you want to." It wasn't a question.

"No, I don't." The look of skepticism was easy to read on Sadie's face. "Look, he's just here because he feels guilty or something. And he might be assigned to look after me until Jeremiah and Jonathan are found."

Sadie shook her head. "I'm sure he does feel some guilt, and he should. He was a dick. But, Milena, he doesn't have to protect you. The Feds can assign someone else to you. There are thousands of law enforcement officers in this city. Any one of them can protect you."

Milena blocked out the common sense her friend was using. "He's arrogant to the nth degree. He strode into the house and practically told me I was his...like a caveman or something. He thinks that throwing money at me and putting me on his insurance will fix everything."

Sadie shifted until she was lying on her side and her head was propped up by a hand. She was about as different from Milena as she could get. Her dark auburn hair fell messily around her shoulders and her green eyes were piercing in their intensity. She was almost five inches taller than Milena, and slender in a way Milena would never be.

"Let me tell you something about dominant men...once they decide they want something, they're gonna get it one way or another."

Milena shook her head. "That's not how things work."

"It is," Sadie insisted. "Let me guess, he told you he left for your own good, right?"

"Yeah, pretty much."

"Men like TJ have crazy high standards for themselves. It's ridiculous, really. They think they have to be perfect. I'm guessing he was really good at what he did in the Army..." Sadie's voice trailed off, as if she was asking a question without coming out and actually voicing it.

Milena nodded. "Yeah, I got that impression. He was a sniper."

"Oh Christ," Sadie murmured, and turned to flop onto her back. "Yeah, so he was probably *very* good at his job. He got hurt and was sent home...to him, I'm sure that felt like a massive failure. He was frustrated he wasn't over there still fighting, and then he was chaptered out of the service altogether. When he had healed enough, he lived with you, right?"

"He didn't have anywhere else to go," Milena told her friend defensively.

"Don't you get it?" Sadie asked. "There he was, still healing, no home, no job, he probably felt like he'd let his friends and country down. He was lost. I'm frankly surprised he stayed as long as he did."

Milena couldn't help but flinch. That hurt.

"Oh sweetie," Sadie said, and leaned over and put her hand on Milena's knee. "I didn't mean that in a bad way. What I meant was that he *had* to have loved you to have stayed for as long as he did. He left because he didn't feel like he was man enough for you. He was trying to be noble. Men like him don't like to feel vulnerable. At all."

"I didn't judge him, Sadie. Not for one second. I would've been there by his side as he worked through whatever he had to, but he didn't give me the chance."

Sadie turned back over and stared at the ceiling once more. "You have to be sneaky with men like him," she informed her friend. "They need your support, but you have to do it in such a way that they don't really realize what you're doing. He's got a group of close friends, right?"

"I have no idea."

"He does," Sadie said with conviction. "His tribe. And I'll bet those friends have women of their own. You need to get to know them. Get close to them. They'll be your source of support when it comes to your man because TJ isn't going to come home and tell you when he's had a bad day. You'll be able to sense it, but he won't tell you why. And that's okay, but you can talk to the other women to help yourself deal with how he is. You can set up guys' nights out. Let him blow off some steam. Cook him dinner. Initiate sex. Let him take you how he wants and needs. *That's* how you help a man like TJ."

"How do you know all this? You're single!"

Sadie smiled up at the ceiling. "I'm a good observer. My aunt married a man just like TJ. Well, maybe not *just* like him, but close enough. You know I was the administrative assistant for McKay-Taggart. Everyone who works there is just like your man. Alpha, obsessive, insanely jealous, and when they fall for someone, they fall *hard*. And it might look like the men are in charge, but ultimately, it's the women who hold most of the power. I've seen my uncle leave in the middle of an important meeting because my aunt called and needed something. He's big, and sometimes scary, but my aunt and his kids mean the world to him."

Milena sighed. She wanted to believe her friend, but it was so hard. "He let me down, Sadie. Big time. I don't know that I'll ever be able to trust him again."

"You will," Sadie said with conviction.

On behalf of 1001 Dark Nights,

Liz Berry and M.J. Rose would like to thank ~

Steve Berry
Doug Scofield
Kim Guidroz
Jillian Stein
InkSlinger PR
Dan Slater
Asha Hossain
Chris Graham
Fedora Chen
Kasi Alexander
Jessica Johns
Dylan Stockton
Richard Blake
BookTrib After Dark
and Simon Lipskar

Made in United States
North Haven, CT
28 December 2023

46575731R00083